CW00859789

Once Upon A Broken Dream

Once Upon A Broken Dream

A Collection of Short Stories

Edited by Natalie J Case

Acknowledgments

I want to thank all of my fellow authors for trusting me with your stories, and for taking a leap of faith on a new idea. Also, a big thank you to Miika Hannila and Creativia for letting me run with this.

I also need to thank all of the many people who have encouraged my writing, especially those who helped me spread my wings and helped me think and create outside the world I lived in.

And a big thank you to all of the writers out there who helped me hone my editing chops by letting me hack away at their stories.

Forward

This project began as an idea I had, something I took from some writing class or seminar I've taken over the years. With a base of writers as diverse as Creativia boasts, I knew that we could end up with an amazing group of stories that all began with a single premise.

I gave the writers a prompt and then gave them free reign to interpret that prompt in any genre, in any style, to tell any story that the prompt inspired. The result is this collection of stories that journey through science fiction, steampunk, paranormal, fantasy, horror and more. It includes stories that teach us a lesson, introduce us to new worlds, lift us up and leave us wondering.

The prompt all of the writers began with was, "Her/his life was no fairy-tale. There was no prince(ess), no talking animals, no happily ever after." In some of these stories that prompt is easy to spot. In others, it's more the theme of the piece. Either way, it's an eclectic group of stories that I hope you all enjoy.

I feel I should issue a warning here, that not all the stories in this mix have happy endings, and there is one that deals with suicidal ideation (It All Comes Down) and another that contains a violent rape and murder (The Ginger Man).

Contents

Sapphire Heartbreaks

by Richard M. Ankers

An unpleasant evening for an unpleasant pursuit, Britannia echoed the mood of its ruler Queen Victoria: stormy; dark and ever brooding. In a seedy part of London ill-befitting their quarry, Mortimer Headlock, investigator extraordinaire and detective to The Crown, and his often accomplice, the beautiful Miss Grace Grace, are stood in the torrential rain. Neither are best pleased.

"Rainstorms are meant for ducks and deserters, not English gentlemen." The shadow lifted his dark collar and backed away from the dripping gutters and globular gaslights; the alleyway swallowed him in deepest night.

"I told you to bring an umbrella," quipped a voice of honeyed silk.

"That is a parasol, Grace, not an umbrella."

"Same difference, Mortimer."

"Speaking as a man, far from it. And this area is unsafe enough to someone of my profession without drawing unnecessary attention through aquamarine accessories."

"Grump."

"Realist."

"Working by your philosophies, I should imagine this hellhole more dangerous to me than you. I am a lady, you know."

Grace batted her long, dark eyelashes although the darkness precluded the sparkling mischief beneath them.

"Hm, lady, you say."

Grace prodded her associate with said parasol and grinned not unlike Mister Carroll's Cheshire cat.

Mortimer Headlock was a man used to working alone, in silence, with nothing but his own thoughts and perhaps a sandwich. Yet, Miss Grace Grace, so good her father, Professor Grace, named her twice, provided a distraction he found welcome despite the rain, wind and midwinter misery they currently frequented. Her canary-yellow self, a colour she always wore regardless of the weather, never failed to bring a little sunshine into his day, or in this case, night.

"Why don't you tell me exactly why we're here as seen as whatever we're here for is not," Grace purred snapping Headlock from his daydream.

"How can you be so sure it is not?"

"You're looking this way."

"Ah, as astute as ever."

"So?"

"It might be best if you don't. Vicky was specific."

"Vicky?"

"Her majesty Queen Victoria, Empress of India and ruler of the whole the Britannian Empire."

"Queen Victoria should have sufficed."

"I like to be exact." Headlock looked away to hide his smile.

"May I speak candidly?" said Grace leaning in conspiratorially.

"Please do."

"If you do not tell me why I am stood outside in the pouring rain at near midnight, regardless of what Her Majesty wishes, you might find yourself extracting a parasol from somewhere inappropriate the next time you visit the latrine." Grace stamped her booted foot for extra effect making a point to angle the splashed water toward her companion.

"Well, if you put it like that."

"I do."

Headlock inhaled as though resurfacing after a near drowning, beckoned Grace and her parasol to his side, whilst making quite sure he could still see the terrace houses opposite their hidey-hole.

"I have spent the last three weeks, weekends and all, camped out at this spot at Vicky's, I mean Her Majesty's, request."

"Ooh, I'm intrigued," Grace cooed.

"Shh!" whispered Headlock. "Anyhow, as I was saying."

"Sorry." Grace zipped her lips.

"The man charged with maintaining Her Majesty's — alterations."

Grace shivered at Headlock's description. "You're talking about Robert Swift the inventor."

"Yes."

Grace nodded, then gestured for him to continue.

"Since Her Majesty's alterations, she has become somewhat attuned to the world around her. Amazing actually, but that is a story for another day. Regardless, it was Her Majesty who realised the man who maintains her was being followed."

"Did he himself not notice?"

"No."

"Not at all?"

"Not a clue, apparently. Neither do I that he's actually here; he is an elusive soul. I have lost him nightly, which irks. In the circumstances, regardless of where he may or may not be, though I suspect, it is best he stays metaphorically in the dark. Master Swift is delicate, to say the least, and no stranger to the poppy. And yes, before you ask, Grace, I have checked The Bohemia opium house prior to here. In both mine and Her Majesty's humble opinions, such a shock to his already frail constitution might result in something both he and she regrets."

"I see," said Grace.

Headlock saw by her furrowed brow, she did.

"I have been charged with finding out who follows him and why. Each night for the period I have mentioned, I have trailed him to his door."

"And."

"He enters, then nothing: no lights; no sounds; no signs of life whatsoever."

"Apart from his visitor."

"Exactly."

"So, why me?"

"His shadow spooks."

"You are certain it is someone working alone."

"Of that, I cannot be certain, but it is only ever a lone spy."

"You have seen them?"

"I have been as close as you and I are now."

"And?"

"I lost it."

"You!"

"Shh!"

"But, Mortimer, you are the greatest of your kind. If they might evade you, then what chance has anyone else of capturing them. If you have chosen me for speed, I really should have worn different footwear."

Headlock pulled a face and shifted in his stance; rainwater poured from his bowler. "I am not making a very good job of this, Grace. The whole episode troubles me."

Headlock's hand shot out to catch the elbow of the gleaming beauty that was Miss Grace Grace. His words had staggered her in a way sights so extraordinary as to shock the hardest of men had not. In his way, he did not blame her.

"Thank you, Mortimer," Grace said once she'd got ahold of herself. "It is just I am unused to you being troubled. I thought nothing could."

"Well, something has. I cannot put it into words other than this: I need help. Female help. I could think of no one I should rather have at my side in this most unusual scenario than you." Headlock attempted a smile but the miserable conditions washed it away.

"Of course, I'm flattered, honoured even, but I still do not see?"

"You will, Grace, and soon."

Headlock put a gloved finger to his lips and pulled his companion close, lowering her parasol in the process and taking a step in front of her to best conceal her yellow self. Grace soon saw why.

The figure came out of the night like a boulder on wheels. Moving with the steady motions of a languid ice-skater who'd overfilled on pudding for years at a time, the figure made menace of the almost derelict surroundings. Darker than the terraced brickwork, if not for the rain that bounced off its broad shoulders one might almost have mistaken it for a kiosk or a seaside chalet rather than a human being. The person, head withdrawn into its neck to protect against the elements, made its way along the cobbles; there was no pavement, until reaching the least decrepit house in the street.

Headlock hadn't realised Grace held his hand until she squeezed it. When the giant glanced their way, she squeezed harder.

Giving Grace a slight tap on the shoulder, he pulled her even further into the side street so their backs were almost against the mildewed brickwork. Yet even from their diminished viewpoint, their expected guest's sapphire eyes, gleaming like jewels even in the almost pitch-black, cast a vibrant blue across the deserted street. Like twin lighthouse beams made of a tropical sky, those eyes scanned for them. Only when certain it was alone, did it turn back to the terrace house and press its nose up to the window glass; it chinked.

"Those eyes," said Grace. "I cannot describe them."

"I told you it was hard to explain," whispered Headlock.

"Glasses?" asked Grace.

"I don't think so."

"Could it be one of these new-fangled automata? I have seen such hulks piloting, or rather powering with their incredible strength, the Pegasus Carriages that fill London's daytime skies."

"No, they have no eyes nor need for them."

"Then what?"

"In some way, they are their host's actual eyes but enhanced. What's more, I suspect them deaf, as once its gaze is averted it is almost totally oblivious to anyone around it. As I stated, I approached them so close as to touch, and not once did it detect me."

"You mean approached him, not it. That's twice you've addressed him as such. It must be a him, as an it cannot operate without instruction."

"I always mean what I say."

Grace pulled a face; Headlock remained unmoved.

Edging closer again, the two observed the behemoth, for at such close proximity there was no other word for it. The giant swayed back and forth like a willow in a summer breeze silent as the grave despite its cumbersome shell.

"It searches," said Headlock. "It seeks our man. Every night the same."

If Grace was to respond, the imminent clatter of horse's hooves prevented it. Like some reckless charge of the Light Brigade, three speeding Hansom Cabs, more charioteers, or drunks, than reputable horsemen, shot past in a blur of dark shapes and foul language. When the proverbial dust of their passage settled, the giant had gone.

"Damn it all!"

"Shh!" hissed Grace.

One velvet-gloved finger had pressed itself to Headlock's lips before he could argue, another steered his vision back from the coachmen to the supposedly deserted house.

"The curtains," Grace whispered.

There were no questions, no whats or ifs, Headlock knew Grace too well. He turned his eyes back upon the house and spied what anger had prevented: a twitch in the fabric of the night.

"Swift," said Headlock. "Not so lost, after all."

Sliding along the mildewed wall, Headlock skipped across the alleyway, then beckoned Grace to follow. There the two waited in silence, and waited, and waited.

Headlock had learned long ago that patience was the key to practical investigating. Senses honed over years, through notable adventures such as the Shangri-La incident and worse, had taught him that time was always the key. The seconds turned to minutes, then hours and still he remained gargoyle-like. Distant church bells rang midnight, one, two and more. Grace to her credit did the same even suppressing her normal urge to ask questions for this was no time for them. They were the hunters who'd lost one quarry and sought another; he obliged.

Even in a full-length coat and wrapped for the season, Robert Swift was a man slender of body, yet still sharp of mind; he was more cautious than a cat. Only when sure of his isolation did he traipse off into the night head bowed, bowler hat balanced upon his head.

"Is he always so stooped?" asked Grace.

"No," a terse response.

The second Swift disappeared around the corner, Headlock was at the man's door, his own nose almost touching the floor.

"Gads!"

"What?"

"The cobbles," hissed Headlock.

"What about them?"

"They're cracked."

"So?"

"They weren't before."

"Oh, my!" gasped Grace.

A gesture to follow him and Headlock was off like a shot. And so the hunt began.

London was a city of twists and turns, water and stone, and Robert Swift made a circuitous route utilising all that cover to the full. Headlock, however, was no ordinary thief or vagabond intent on a gentleman's purse; he was a man of purpose and professionalism. A ghost would not have known itself followed such stealth did Headlock employ. Grace followed in his wake equally skilled in the hunt, a girl to be reckoned with. The two pursued Robert Swift here and there, the inventor in a constant state of nervousness, his twitching as much a part of him as his shoes.

For almost an hour, the two companions followed he who Her Majesty had claimed followed himself until reaching Highgate Cemetery and a gap in the iron railings to enter it.

Headlock went first following the still wary inventor, Grace next. The rain came down heavier then, if it were possible; Swift seemed not to notice. It was Grace who pointed at the man, her intention all too evident.

"Yes, he's more relaxed now," said Headlock, his first words since the cobbles outside their quarry's home.

A great rumble of thunder split the heavens followed by a flash of lightning so intense as to illuminate the whole planet. Swift appeared not to notice as he jinked his way through the haphazard tombstones.

Signaling Grace to pause, Headlock pointed at a memorial larger than the others nestled between two warped oaks, which both took residence behind; Swift had stopped.

The inventor had removed his hat and wrung it between his hands like a naughty child might its favourite teddy bear.

Headlock look puzzled as another bolt of light made daytime of the graves. He pointed at his eyes and then Swift.

"He's weeping," whispered Grace.

"Profusely."

The two edged a touch closer until Swift was clear to see. The man wept oceans enough for all the people of the world and before him the reason why.

It was a tombstone taller than a man, almost as tall and broad as a kiosk or a seaside chalet, one might have said.

"It is a golem, a clockwork golem," Grace whispered in Headlock's ear, as two sapphire eyes lit the creature's would-be head, its gentle ticking audible despite the storm.

There, before the world's foremost man of action might move, Grace did.

In a swirl of canary-yellow and an upraised parasol, she sashayed her way to the distraught inventor's side and placed an arm around his shoulders. Headlock watched on. The girl whispered something to the man who fell to his knees. Grace then did something stranger still, she looked to the tombstone poor Swift had collapsed before, paced to the giant with the sapphire eyes, smiled, then kissed it on what approximated its cheek. She said something in its almost-ear, whereupon it turned and lurched away.

There Grace remained just stood in the pouring rain until the thing had long gone.

Only when Mortimer Headlock and Miss Grace Grace had delivered the inventor back to his home, assisted in packing his suitcase, then seen him to Charing Cross Station and waved him goodbye, did they speak.

"It was his wife."

"Deceased wife," Headlock corrected.

"There are varying degrees of death, Mortimer. For two lovers who refused to part even when the afterlife strove to tear them asunder, there would be no fairytale, no happily ever after, but, perhaps, something else. I think that's all one could ever ask for."

"And I presume that train will take him to her, wherever she's gone, and away from Her Majesty."

"A woman scorned, Mortimer. Robert Swift through clockwork gears and the unknown has given his once dead wife what Her Majesty desires above all else, immortality. We could never have allowed her to acquire it."

"We will never see him again, then?"

"I doubt it. He only needed the push. Correction, they only needed the push."

"So tell me, my dear, what did you say to him out there in the rain?"

"I asked if he still loved her."

"His reply?"

"Almost as much as she loved him. She could not stay away, my friend, although I suspect you already knew this."

Headlock smiled.

"As I have said, dearest Grace, there are things only a woman can make right."

It was Grace's turn to smile. "Are you going to tell Her Majesty?" she asked.

"I doubt there'll be any need."

Mortimer Headlock cast his eyes to the lightening sky, a new dawn just beginning, and the Pegasus Carriages, their spotlights streaming, already illuminating London's streets and rooftops."

Headlock sniffed.

"Is she so mad?" said Grace.

"More so?" replied Headlock offering her his arm.

The End

About the Author: Richard M Ankers

Richard M. Ankers is the author of The Eternals Series published by Creativia. A former Authonomy gold medalist, Richard has appeared in such notable publications as DailyScienceFiction, Devolution Z, Phantaxis and counts himself privileged to have appeared in many others. Richard writes daily for his own self-titled website and loves nothing more than running with a view, whilst dreaming up new storylines for his readers.

Books by Richard Ankers:
The Eternals (Book One in The Eternals Series)
Hunter Hunted (Book Two in The Eternals Series)
Into Eternity (Book Three in The Eternals Series)

Links:
Facebook: https://www.facebook.com/richardmankers/
Twitter: https://twitter.com/Richard_Ankers
Website: https://richardankers.com/

Suzanne Goes to Market

By Susan-Alia Terry

Suzanne stepped out of the portal, wobbled to a nearby bench and sat down. A brightly colored, child's beach bucket was shoved into her lap.

"You gonna hurl, you hurl into that." Bobby Sunshine said before crossing his arms and staring at her as if daring her to follow-through. Suzanne's impulse was to roll her eyes and flip him the bird, but she was still too queasy, all she could do was close her eyes, grab the bucket and breathe.

"I'm fine, I'm not gonna hurl." She told him. Teleporting was totally cool, but it made her want to puke. The key, she learned, was to pretend like it didn't, but until she could pull that off, she'd have to put up with the teasing — and the bucket.

"Yeah, well you don't look it. My shift's almost over, and I swear to god if I have to stay late to clean up your puke... You may be our Lord's consort, but your puke is as nasty as everyone else's."

One opened eye showed him grinning at her. She closed that eye and flipped him the bird. His cackling laugh made her smile. Suzanne liked Bobby, he reminded her of Big Tom from her neighborhood. Like Big Tom, Bobby was a tall, lanky, aging rocker type that treated her like a princess, (although now she pretty much was one). Every time she saw him, she wanted to ask about his name, but that really wouldn't fly. Clan names were personal, they had meaning, and like being in a gang, if you weren't down, you didn't get to know. She might have been a member of the Clan, but she certainly wasn't down. If she was, she might have gotten a new name of her own.

Suzanne opened her eyes and shoved the bucket back at him. "I said I was fine."

"Uh huh, whatever," Bobby said, taking the bucket and still looking unconvinced. His bearded face scrunched in a frown. "What're you doing here alone? Does he know you're here?"

"Who do you think sent me?" She regretted the bite in her voice the minute the words were out of her mouth. It wasn't Bobby's fault. "I'm sorry, I just hate this fucking place."

Bobby folded his long body onto the bench beside her and stared out of the small alcove into Clan Air's section of The City. When he spoke, he pitched his voice low to minimize the echo. "Listen, the transition is hard, I know. But it'll get easier."

She scoffed, couldn't help herself. When was it supposed to get easy? She'd already been a vampire for about as long as she'd been human — sixteen, going on seventeen years — and nothing was easy! When exactly was she supposed to start to feel like she belonged?

"You're thinking like a human, it's still your instinct, but it's just the remnants of your humanity getting in the way — as my Master liked to say. It'll go away. I can't tell you when because it's different for all of us, but I just know that it will. Hang in there, it'll all start to make sense."

Suzanne was afraid to look him in the eye. If she did, the "remnants of her humanity" would take over and she'd pour out all the fear and uncertainty she carried around without an outlet. "Why do you care?" She asked instead.

Bobby shrugged. "I like you. You got me all protective."

She sighed but said nothing. He sat with her until hurling was completely off the table, and then she got up and walked though the alcove and into The City.

* * *

Suzanne hated being in The City, and would happily never set foot in it ever again for the rest of her life. Waking up and finding out vampires were real because she'd become one, was freaky enough. But then finding out that there were walking, talking creatures she'd never heard of living in a hot, filthy, underground cavern — that was a whole other world of *Fuck, No*. But Lord Lugan, her Master and husband — *husband was the same as consort, right?* — had sent her down here to buy a slave. Of course, he could send literally anyone but he chose *her*. What did she know about buying slaves? Not a damn thing. It would serve him right if she brought back a bad one, but Suzanne couldn't do that. She would try to make a good choice because she needed to make him happy, even though her very existence made him want to pick on her — or worse.

The slave market was in the middle of The City — this wasn't going to be a quick in-and-out, like a stop at the corner store. Suzanne bit the inside of her cheek and inched forward, joining the crowd, and trying not to let any of these *things* accidentally touch her. The place was a damn horror show. Fucking man-sized insects, and fuzzy things with *oh fuck that's a tentacle* — she ducked down an alley with a repressed scream. Walking the streets of New York she felt like such a bad ass, but down here she was just a punk wishing for a bucket of bleach and a can of Raid.

A loud cheer came from somewhere nearby. Curiosity about whatever could be that exciting overruled her disgust and she set out again. Scooting through the crowd, when she got close enough to the source of the commotion she managed to duck through an opening to find herself near the front of a large circled off area.

"Place yer bets! Place yer bets! Big Poppa is back! You thought he was down, but he's not out! He's two and two! Can he make that three? Place yer bets!" A half-man half-animal wearing a skirt was shouting and indicating something that could be human, except that it was a dark red color, extremely muscular and at least eight or nine feet tall. It walked around in circles, posing while the crowd cheered. "Or will this challenging MoFo rip Big Poppa a new one? Can you dig it? Place yer bets!" The challenger was a little shorter and not as muscular, with a huge pointed head and a mouth full of jagged teeth. When the crowd booed, it opened its mouth wider and let out a growl.

"Place yer bets!" The animal-man continued to shout, walking around the crowd and shaking a large pouch. He was pretty damn hot from the waist up — ripped, with a perfect six-pack. Suzanne both wanted and didn't want to know what he looked like under that skirt, but those furry legs and hoofed feet probably meant that it wasn't pretty. Her pocket buzzed and she started and yelped in surprise. A group of feathered somethings stared at her with beady black eyes as she fumbled in her pocket, embarrassed. Once her fingers closed around the disk she remembered that there was no switch on the thing, and chuckled, trying to play it off. Other-kin (which now included her), liked to use magic for all sorts of things. The smooth stone disk, about the size of a

13

quarter and maybe twice as thick, was a magical watch — it vibrated every 30 minutes. It wasn't like watches didn't work in The City; Lugan was just being a dick when he gave it to her. He'd given her two hours to get to The City, buy the slave, and get back. A half-hour just passed. She didn't have time to watch some weird wrestling match — or whatever the fuck this was — which was disappointing because she had no idea that shit like this went on down here, and now really wanted to stay and watch. But she had to get moving.

* * *

As she approached a nearby doorway, the scent of cooking meat hung heavily in the air and made her mouth water. After she was made, Suzanne had found out that real vampires weren't undead but were mortal just like everything else. They could eat human food — in fact, it helped them to blend in and appear human — but they couldn't live off of it. She knew her body was reacting because she was hungry, not because she wanted to eat the meat. She was just always hungry, and it didn't matter how many times she told Lugan, he refused to listen. He was over seven hundred years old, and could go *weeks* without feeding. To him, she was just being greedy: "*You are young, and the blood intoxicates. It is not nourishment you crave, but the power of the blood.*" Which sounded like so much bullshit to her. Vampire or human, hungry was hungry — it meant she needed to eat.

The restaurant was just a hole in the wall — literally. Creeping closer, she peeked in. All these places served blood — on tap, no less. Suzanne could feed until she was finally full, and Lugan would never know. She pulled the pouch of "money" he had given her out of her purse and rifled through it. How much would it cost? How much would a slave cost? She had no idea on both counts. There could be enough here for one or both with possibly some left over. The smell, combined with her hunger and potential disobedience, made her antsy — could she take the chance? Her feet decided she would.

Her defiance had wilted by the time she sat down at the rough table.

A grey, stumpy, elephant-looking thing shuffled over and sniffed at her. "Blood." It grunted. The sores on its face, made Suzanne gag, and almost change her mind. Almost.

She nodded her head and tried to be nonchalant. *It's gonna ask for money. It's gonna ask for money. Please let me have enough.* The waiter sniffed at her again before walking away and disappearing into a back room she hadn't noticed before. It returned a short time later carrying a large metal goblet. "Two." It grunted again after placing the goblet on the table. She had to gulp to keep from drooling.

Two what? Suzanne opened her pouch and dumped some of the contents on the counter. *Fuck it.*

The elephant-thing looked at her and then picked out two small crystals — *diamonds?* — and sniffed at her again before walking away. Funny thing, back in Brooklyn she would never let anyone know how much money she had on her. But this wasn't Brooklyn and her money pouch was filled with glass, clay, and metal beads, pins (both safety and decorative), gem stones (cut and uncut), pebbles, and polished coins from the surface. How the hell was she supposed to know what it wanted?

Once the pouch was secured back in her purse, Suzanne picked up the goblet. It was warm. The blood was fresh, and she barely tasted it before it was all gone. She had to force herself to stop licking the inside and straining her tongue to reach the remains at the bottom. Having another was an easy decision — one more and then she'd be on her way.

She had three more. Suzanne was full by the third, but she had a fourth for insurance. The "price" had varied wildly each time: For the second glass, it wanted five coins and a safety pin. The third cost a larger crystal and a pebble. For the fourth it took two clay beads and four metal ones. It was hunger, but mostly uncertainty, that kept her mouth shut throughout. What was done was done; she just hoped she still had enough for the slave.

Suzanne was just leaving the restaurant when the disk in her pocket buzzed again. *Shit!* She only had an hour left. But the good thing was that the blood had calmed her nerves. Her surroundings were a little less disgusting, and she felt more at home in her skin. Feeling better, she picked up the pace — wanting to get this over with as soon as possible.

* * *

The slave market offered more variety than she bargained for; naked and dirty humans of every race and age were stuffed in cages, waiting to be sold. Suzanne wandered around for what felt like an eternity, unable to choose and not knowing what she wanted. Lugan had given her absolutely no clues — "*I don't care what you get,"* he had said as he placed the money pouch and disk in her hands. *"Just get one. Be back in two hours."* Then he'd walked away. He was *like that whenever he talked to her,* if he bothered to talk to her that is.

Whenever Suzanne thought of him, and what they had, she couldn't help but feel cheated. Being a vampire was totally cool and she wouldn't go back to being human, but she'd never asked for this life. One minute she'd snuck out of her parent's house to get a smoke, and the next she was waking up a vampire. Not just any vampire either, but the bride of a king! She had seen all the movies: *He had walked the earth for centuries until he found his perfect companion for eternity.* What could possibly be more romantic than that?

Except that it was a lie.

When she woke up, the first thing he did after explaining things, and giving her a bit of blood, was smack her across the room. Turns out that her new husband was a mean, nasty, son of a bitch.

But why? Seriously, how do you pick someone to spend eternity by your side and then treat them like shit?

The answer finally came in the form of an old and faded photograph she'd found one day when she was avoiding Lugan and exploring a different section of their compound. If there was one thing that Suzanne had a lot of, it was free time, and the best way she could spend it, was away from him. It was an out-of-sight, out-of-mind thing. If he didn't see her, or ask to see her, he didn't beat on her. Simple.

The picture was of Lugan and a woman wearing old-fashioned clothes. He was in a suit, and she was in a high-collared white blouse with poufy sleeves and a dark skirt. She stood next to him with her hand on his left shoulder. Lugan was sitting on his throne staring at the camera — he looked so suave and handsome. Although Suzanne had never gone for black guys when she was human, even back then she would have agreed that he was good looking. But it was the woman that fascinated her — she was petite, with long dark hair, pale skin, and eyes almost too close together, which gave her an exotic look. It was uncanny how much she and the woman looked alike — they could be twins. Handwritten in fading ink on the back was: *Lugan + Cassandra 1893.* Asking Lugan about it earned her five broken fingers — he wasn't talking.

Cassandra. Who was she?

Her Clan mates were happy to fill her in, especially since they knew why Lugan chose her. The ones eager to talk seemed amused that she would now be in on the joke. Cassandra was Lugan's ex-consort who'd been exiled for misconduct with a slave. (They said *misconduct* like she'd know what the hell they were talking about, and Suzanne had been too afraid to say otherwise. So much of her current life was spent pretending she knew something when she didn't.) The juicy, and scandalous part though, was that Lugan *exiled* her instead of killing her outright. It was hard for anyone who knew him to believe that he was capable of mercy, but it only went to prove how deeply and passionately in love he actually was. On anyone else in his position, that show of mercy would have been considered a weakness, but they allowed him that one flaw because he was not known to be sentimental. He had never taken a consort before he met Cassandra and he even went so far as to dismiss the idea of love and to make fun of anyone who believed in it. Cassandra had changed that, had changed *him*. They'd been together for over two hundred years and so her disloyalty hit him hard. He was bitter and hated her for betraying him, and that, Suzanne found out, was where she came in. Her resemblance to Cassandra wasn't a coincidence. She had been chosen all right, but her happily ever after had a catch. She was a stand-in. Every time Lugan looked at her, he saw Cassandra. Every punch, every cruel word, every broken bone, was payback. Suzanne knew that he didn't actually hate her, because he *didn't know who she was*. But that was little comfort. Lugan liked to say that they were together until 'death do them part'. Suzanne was very clear on whose death that would be.

* * *

After circling the market a few times, Suzanne found herself lingering in front of a pen of kids. If she got a young one, they could grow into the job, and Lugan would get his money's worth, right? Plus, the whole "slave" thing was easier to think about with kids. The adults gave her the heebees. She could order a kid around, no problem.

"Young ones can be very useful. Heh heh heh." The yellow-eyed, snaggle-toothed, and pointy-eared monster said as it came to stand next to her. "Give you many years of service. Heh heh heh."

"How much for the boy?" She asked, pointing at a skinny blonde boy of about nine or ten. The now smiling monster stepped into her personal space, causing her to step back.

"Good choice! Heh heh heh. He will be very strong. Heh heh heh." It said, its moist, nasty breath forcing her to take another step back. "The price, a pittance really, is inconsequential for one such as yourself. Heh. Heh. Heh." It said, closing the gap between them again.

Oh for fuck's sake. That laugh was simultaneously creeping her out and getting on her nerves. She stepped back. The disk buzzed again. She did not have time for this! Pulling out her pouch, Suzanne poured some of its contents into her palm and then held it out. The monster grinned at her and then took the four largest cut red stones. It then turned and made a string of those "heh" sounds at another nearby who unlocked the cage.

"You will be needing a leash and collar. Heh heh heh."

Suzanne stuck her palm out again and sighed. *You gonna rip me off for that too?* It took a few coins. Probably the only time down here when she didn't overpay for something. If Lugan was going to send her on these little trips, he was going to have to teach her the money.

* * *

With the slave trotting along behind her, the plan was to make a bee-line for the exit. Until she spotted Kai. Suzanne had only been a member of the Clan for a short time, but she'd heard of Kai, he was the Clan's most infamous member. She had never actually seen him before, but his description made him unmistakable — medium height and build, light brown skin, long black hair, and a tribal tattoo on his face, curving down his neck. The description didn't do him justice though. In person, he was sexy in that dark, bad-boy kind of way. Like the guys she used to go for before.

She followed his progress as he moved past the stalls. He stopped at one, picked up something and examined it. The entire city had a flea market vibe; everywhere Suzanne looked there was all kinds of junk for sale. Since she knew next to nothing about him, she was intrigued as to what he found interesting, and maneuvered closer trying to get a look.

For a reason that her Clan mates didn't know, Lugan and Kai hated each other. All anyone knew was that their maker Aram, had hippy-dippy ideas about life that Kai bought into, and Lugan didn't. Supposedly, Kai didn't even feed off humans, and gave himself to Lucifer to punish himself for all the wild shit he had done back in the day. He was much older than Lugan and should be Clan Leader, but he'd turned his back on the Clan and didn't contest when Lugan took over. From what she could tell, the Clan was set against him — he had abandoned them after all. But that didn't mean that behind closed doors he wasn't a source of fascination, and a little envy. Suzanne didn't know what to make of him, and like most of the others she was curious.

She watched him a little longer, he eventually purchased something, but she was still too far way to see what it was. Finally, she forced her eyes away, she really had to get going, get this kid back to... *fuck!* Suzanne had been so focused on Kai that she'd dropped the leash, and the kid had wandered away. *Where are you, you little... There!* Her eyes found him, he was now staring longingly at the meats hanging from a pole in a stall across the market, and Kai was a few feet away on a direct path toward him. *No, no no!* She couldn't get the slave and not speak to Kai, and if she spoke to him...? Nobody from the clan had actually spoken to Kai in ages. He was like a ghost, they gossiped about him, but it was done in secret after making doubly sure Lugan was nowhere around. This was bad, so fucking bad. What if she just said to hell with it and ran? *Dammit!* She'd been feeling all full of herself too. Braving this dirty, smelly place, sneaking some blood, actually getting the stupid slave... She'd even thought that since she'd done everything he asked, that maybe Lugan would be nice to her for a while!

She checked the distance again, maybe she could grab the kid and go? *Fuck it.* She took off across the marketplace. When she was within arms reach of the kid, Kai still hadn't seemed to notice her. *Yes! I'm gonna make it.*

She grabbed the boy, picked up the leash and moved him bodily in the other direction. That was a mistake. The startled boy screamed and started to cry. Now they were causing a scene.

"Greetings, Cousin."

Fuck!

"Lord Kai," Suzanne said with a bow, before panic made her mind go blank. It also dilated her pupils and dropped her fangs. *Great.* She still had no control of the response, and was unable to will her features back to normal. Her face was stuck that way until she calmed down. Embarrassed, she kept her eyes at his waist, until she realized what she was looking at and forced them to the floor at his feet. *Tell him your name, stupid.* "Um, sorry, uh, my name is...Suzanne." *And I'm an idiot, nice to meet you.*

"It's a pleasure to meet you, Suzanne." He lightly touched her chin. "Don't worry, you'll eventually be able to control it." She peeked up at him, and to her great relief, he seemed amused. She snatched that moment to study his face. He was so beautiful, but he looked tired. Exhausted really. It was all around his eyes.

The boy chose that moment to give a particularly loud wail, causing her to break her stare. She tugged on the leash. "I swear to god, if you don't shut up!" She warned, distantly realizing that she sounded like her mother, which was disturbing given the circumstances.

"He's hungry, you should feed him." Kai said, looking at the child. She took that moment to examine his face again — why was he so tired? Slowly, he brought his eyes back to hers. Caught staring — again — she quickly switched focus.

"I'll take one of those," she told the lizard-thing vendor, while gesturing at a meat stick, and just like every other time, shoved over a handful of money. The creature promptly plucked out two coins and a blue glass bead with a delicate touch of claws. Suppressing a shudder, she snatched her hand back, dumped what was left in her money pouch and put it away. She handed the stick to the boy, and then wrapped her hand around the leash, making sure she wouldn't drop it again.

"You are new to The City, and to handling slaves."

Suzanne would have blushed if she could; although it didn't matter, her stupid face had already betrayed her.

Kai gestured at the lizard-thing. "Their race is called Grist. For the record, you overpaid." He held out his hand to the Grist vendor who sulkily dropped the two coins she had paid into it. He handed them to her. "The key to navigating the market is to know who you are dealing with and what they hold valuable. Grists prefer beads; he took those pesos to trade. Also, there are no set prices, the price of anything is determined by what you're willing to part with." He winked at her. "Learn to haggle." Then he gestured to the boy who was happily munching on whatever kind of meat that was. "You have no idea how much you paid for him, do you?" She shook her head.

"Where is your Master? Why are you here alone?"

God, this was so embarrassing, she felt like a misbehaving teenager. "Lord Lugan is my Master...and um...I'm also his new consort, he sent me to buy the slave." She tried to give a breezy chuckle; it came out sounding like a cough.

"I see." He really looked at her then, making her even more uncomfortable. "Congratulations. How is Lugan?" Things had definitely turned frosty.

"He's good."

"Glad to hear it. Did he tell you specifically to purchase a child?"

"Um, no. He just told me to buy a slave. I just thought…" She shrugged, feeling his disapproval, but unsure how much of it was directed at her for being so stupid.

"Come." He said, and turned and set off toward the slave market. It was a command; she had no choice but to follow.

"It's no big deal." Suzanne said, but his pace didn't slow.

When they reached the pens, one of the monsters hurried over and bowed. Before it opened its mouth, Kai had stepped into its space and began talking in that laughing language. Coming from the monsters, that language was both creepy and annoying. Coming from Kai, it was terrifying. In an instant, he had turned into walking death. Spiders ran up and down her spine and she shivered, intent on him. He never raised his voice, didn't gesture or touch the monster, but it visibly cowered, and for every step Kai took, it took one backwards. Suzanne felt a little lightheaded when she realized that he was helping her out despite his circumstances with Lugan. He was doing this *for her* — she might have fallen in love, just a little, as a result. The monster bowed repeatedly and then took her slave and hurried off.

She wasn't exactly sure when her face changed back.

When Kai spoke again, his demeanor was the same as when they first met, and his voice was casual. "I won't even try to guess at my brother's reasons for sending you here uninformed. Call this a wedding present from me to you. The Clan Leaders have their own arrangements with the goblins for slaves. Should Lugan send you again, you merely have to tell them who you are or who the slave is for. Unless he wants something specific, you'll never have to choose, or pay for them yourself."

It was all Suzanne could do not to hug him.

The goblin — she really did prefer 'monster' — came back leading a female on a leash. The girl looked to be about the same age that Suzanne was when her life had changed.

"Mistakes are sometimes easy to make. Heh heh heh." The goblin reached out to hand her something. "No hard feelings? Heh heh heh," it said as it dropped the coins, and all four cut red stones, back into her palm.

Kai was walking her back to Clan Air's section of The City when the stone in her pocket buzzed. She stopped walking and dug it out and showed it to him.

"I'm *so* screwed. He gave me two hours. The rock buzzed four times."

If Kai and Lugan were on speaking terms, telling Lugan that she was late because she ran into his brother, would be fine. But as it was, she'd pretty much made up her mind not to mention meeting Kai at all. Being late however, would cause him to ask questions.

When he saw the disk, Kai looked surprised at first and then a sly smile spread over his face when he held out his hand.

"Lugan knows modern timepieces are much more reliable." He spat on the rock and rubbed it in while whispering something, and then he handed it back to her. She made a face but took it when his eyes insisted. "The spell is a simple one to confuse." The rock buzzed again when she put it in her pocket.

"I don't get it," she said. It buzzed once more when they started walking again.

He shrugged. "Some magic is flimsy, other magic is strong. Sometimes it's the caster's fault, other times it's just weak magic. If Lugan takes issue with your tardiness, simply show him the stone."

It buzzed again.

The giggle that escaped her was very un-consort-like. "Thanks. Do you know a lot of magic?"

"I've picked up a few things." He said, before gesturing in the general direction of Clan Air's portal. "You can make it the rest of the way?"

"Sure," she said, disappointed that their time together was over.

He placed his palm lightly on her chest and said something she didn't understand.

"I have no idea what you just said." She said, uncomfortable at having to admit it. Lugan and his cronies spoke the vampire language all the time, but he ignored her requests to learn. That was something for the in-crowd, not the likes of her.

"The shortened version, loosely translated is this: May glory find you and stain your lips with the blood of your enemies."

She smiled, "Thank you. For everything."

He smiled in return and she melted a little. "Be well, Suzanne, Consort to Clan Leader Lugan of Clan Air." Then he bowed and walked away into the crowd.

The rock buzzed again.

Suzanne watched him until she could no longer see his dark head in the mass of bodies. There were very few moments that she treasured, especially in her new life. As she walked back to the portal, she went over and over this one, sealing it into her memory.

"Ooh look at you! I'm sure Lord Lugan will be pleased." Bobby Sunshine beamed at her from his post, leaning against the portal entrance.

"I thought your shift was almost over?"

He shrugged. "Vampire time, girl. Vampire time. Let's get you home." He said with a wink.

The rock buzzed again.

She stepped into the portal making sure the slave was beside her; keenly aware of how much she did not want to go 'home'. When the world shifted she remembered a long-forgotten conversation with her mother.

"*All I want out of life is to be happy.*"

"*Who says you get to be happy? Ain't nobody promised happiness in life.*"

The world settled with a jolt, and the slave vomited. Suzanne just managed to keep her stomach, her mother's words stuck on repeat in her head.

"*Ain't nobody promised happiness in life.*"

Bitter tears swelled and she hurriedly tried to blink them away.

The rock buzzed again.

The End

About the Author: Susan-Alia Terry

Susan has always loved to read, but it was only in her late 40's that she discovered a passion for writing. Her genre of choice is Paranormal Fantasy as it allows her to put her unique spin on angels, vampires, werewolves, and the supernatural.

If you enjoyed *Suzanne Goes to Market*, you can read about Kai and his universe in Susan's debut novel, *Coming Darkness*.

When she's not lurking on social media, Susan is diligently working on the follow up to her debut, tentatively titled *Dreaming in Shadow*.

Books by Susan-Alia Terry:
Coming Darkness

Links:
Website: http://susanaliaterry.com/
Facebook: https://www.facebook.com/authorsusanaliaterry
Twitter: https://twitter.com/@susan_alia

"Goodbye"

By Leo Kane

Not everyone looking for a new job finds their career path in a crematorium garden. Not everyone is as fortunate as me.

My life changed on a most miserable Monday, the weather was damp and dismal under stormy spring skies. The atmosphere in my office was equally depressing. I admit that I was extra irritable that day and, to be honest, I hated my job from Monday to Friday, week in and week out, which meant that I spent most evenings searching the internet for a new one.

My phone rang its happy tune, interrupting my pathetic attempt at concentration which despite several cups of black coffee persisted in being absent without permission. Seeing my grandmother's smiling face on the screen, my defiant finger hovered over 'decline' until I lost my nerve and stabbed 'accept' breaking yet another fingernail. Gran spoke gently, something which only happened when she was after something.

"Sue, sweetheart, how are you? I'm fine before you ask. Please can you take me to a funeral service this afternoon? I was going with Dolly from number five, but the old dear had a fall last night. Between you and me I think she likes her gin too much."

I sighed, tucking the mobile between my shoulder and ear while chewing off the remnants of my nail and silently cursing the spreadsheet that demanded my attention. Why did she have to need me today? It was obvious that I wouldn't be able to escape office hell any time soon, so I sat up straight, took a deep breath and said,

"Gran, I'm very busy. We've got to finish the company's year end accounts before the tax man cometh. I'd love to say yes, but I can't get out of work today without causing major problems. I'm sorry."

There was an ominous silence on the ether. Gran was thinking. This call wasn't going to end in my favour. I knew my priorities weren't in the game, but I played out the charade anyway.

She 'who must be obeyed' cleared her throat before in a weak old lady voice designed to gain my sympathy she said, "I know what an important person you are and I wouldn't ask if I didn't absolutely need to, but you're my only grandchild and your feckless parents are off gallivanting in that there Torre-bloodymolinas again, so there's no-one else to ask. Please, Sue."

My mood was so cranky that her pleading exasperated me. I tried my best to be assertive and in a voice much firmer than my resolve said, "The boss will have a blue fit if I leave the office at such short notice on such a busy day. Can't you cadge a lift in one of the funeral cars? What about a taxi?"

"Susan Jean, you know that those vehicles are for family only and I'm not getting in some strange taxi. You hear about dreadful things happening to single women travelling alone. I'm disappointed by your attitude. I didn't expect you, of all people, to let me down."

I felt a headache coming on. I was in trouble; my Sunday name had been trotted out and wouldn't be taken back in until I relented. I'm too easily ma-nipulated, everybody knows I am, even the company cat, but I wasn't ready to roll over. I rallied my pathetic determination and said, "Gran, I hear what you say about the funeral cars, however, the vast majority of taxi drivers are family men and women earning a respectable living. They aren't into granny bashing or sexual shenanigans with the elderly."

"'Susan Jean Stephenson, did your mother not teach you anything? It's dis-graceful to expect an old lady to take her chances on getting a lift with a wrong un." She sniffed. I sighed. When the family name was invoked, resistance was futile.

"OK, I'll try my best to get this afternoon off. What time's the service?"

"Two o'clock at the crematorium chapel. I'll be ready at half-past one."

"Hang on, old woman; I need to check with my boss first."

"Sue, I don't ask for much. You know how much I hate being dependent on other people. Make sure your boss understands how important it is for you to help your old Granny. If you can't manage that simple task, pass him on to me and I'll make sure he gets the message." Imagining the boss versus my grand-mother, I swallowed a reluctant laugh and said, " You win, whatever happens I'll be there at half-one sharp and you'd better be dressed and waiting. Oh, and in case I lose my lousy job over this, you should have your cheque book and pen ready too." When I popped into his luxury office with my request for the afternoon off for a funeral, the boss took his big feet off the mahogany desk and pretended to care.

He said, "Of course you must take your Grandmother to the funeral. This company believes that happy families make happy workers."

He waited for a grateful smile, so I gave him my best impression of one and said, 'How very wise, sir."

He straightened his silk tie and said, "There's no need for you to use your valuable annual leave on this, Sue. It is Sue, isn't it?"

I bit my tongue and nodded. The power-mad fiend I had been answering to for two years looked pleased with his magnificent memory and continued to patronize me.

"Good, good. In return for this favour, Susie, I know you'll hurry back to work after the service, no dawdling with sherry and canapés afterward, and, of course, you can make up the lost time."

He smiled a magnanimous smile and tipped his head to one side. I realised that he was waiting for me to thank him rather than slap him so I said, "Thank you, Sir," like the pathetic, subservient, wage slave I used to be. I left his office appreciating that the boss was truly a prince amongst men, we all thought so.

Work continued to be horrible all morning, it was the kind of hectic yet unproductive misery experienced in offices everywhere; even the photocopier went on a go-slow. I ran myself ragged trying to jolly along my spotty adoles-cent trainee and cajole the soon to be retired old grump who made up our team to show the youngster what to do. I even resorted to pleading with the finance office for help which taught me patience with pointless and painful pursuits proving that no experience is truly wasted.

I missed lunch, and, with no time to spare escaped the office and dashed through the pouring rain to my scrappy old mini-cooper. It needed new wiper blades; driving half-blind wasn't going to be a lot of fun. All in all, that Monday morning had been a tortuous start to what I had no doubt would end up as a disastrous week in Happy Valley Incorporated. I loathed, despised and hated that job.

Cursing my life, the rain and the boss and fighting the groaning gear box and heavy traffic all the way I finally arrived at Gran's apartment. I ran up the rain slicked path under a half-collapsed expensive un-collapsible umbrella. Feeling faint with a mixture of stress and hunger, I found Gran's spare key in my wet pocket and turned it in the lock. Unfortunately, her neighbour, John, pulled the door open from the inside at the same moment I pushed and I almost fell into the hallway.

Smiling at my sudden stumbling, bedraggled appearance, John caught me and set me back on my feet saying, "Hello, lass, I've been talking to your gran but she seems distracted." He looked at his watch and said, "I'm glad you made it, now I must go and get myself ready. I'll meet you at the crematorium."

Deciding to be polite I asked, "Can I give you a lift?"

"No, thank you, I've got my own transport arranged. Look after Eve... I mean, your Gran."

He left in a whiff of tandoori spices that made my empty stomach rumble and sent me straight to Gran's kitchen to steal a chocolate wafer from the ugly teddy shaped biscuit jar. There was no sign of my grandmother there or in the living room. I went back down the narrow hall way and, after a polite knock, stuck my head round her bedroom door. She was sitting in front of a kidney shaped dresser mirror that, like its owner, had seen better days.

"Gran, it's time to leave; are you ready?"

"Hold your horses, Sue, I'm just putting' me lippy on. You've got crumbs on your blouse."

I brushed them off saying, "Thank you, Chief Eagle Eye. Now come along, you don't want to be late."

She was wearing her best frock and a fancy wedding hat. My grandmother was a good-looking woman who didn't do mourning clothes, saying, "Black never suited my personality," and she was right.

I tried to make up for my earlier attitude with a compliment, "Oh, Gran, you look lovely."

She smiled like sunshine then, fixing her eyes on mine in the mirror, said, "Do you remember your granddad Tom's funeral? What a shock we had when they dropped his coffin - I thought my heart stopped." She giggled like a naughty schoolgirl.

"Gran, I had nightmares about that for years, it wasn't funny."

"Ah, Sue, my Tom would've loved it. His brother was to blame; he was drunk like he always was. Not so much a pall-bearer as he was a piss-pot, that one. He fancied me y'know, the dirty little..."

"Grandmother, please, can we go now?"

"Of course we can if you're absolutely sure that you're ready. Do you want to borrow a comb and a lipstick?"

I stuck my tongue out at her reflection and said, "No thanks, but I do need to borrow a brolly."

We huddled under granddad's old golf umbrella and dashed down the path as fast as Gran's arthritic hips and a walking stick would allow. She puffed and panted while I squeezed her into my little car and strapped her soft body in tight. It was like tying a marshmallow to a chair, she didn't raise a finger to help me clearly preferring to give herself up to my tender ministrations. I found myself fantasizing about a different funeral, then feeling a rush of guilt I sent up a silent "I didn't mean it, God, please forgive me," prayer.

Gran hung onto the seat belt for dear life while I managed to achieve a high speed of 25 mph through the same awful weather and traffic that had plagued me earlier. My passenger was oddly silent, I thought she might be scared given the poor visibility, I was a little anxious myself. It never occurred to me that she might be feeling sad. That's how insensitive I used to be. I'm a changed woman now.

We were the last mourners to arrive at the crematorium chapel. The building was a modern monstrosity which, on that wet Monday afternoon, sheltered a miserly scattering of friends and family. The scarcity of people saying their last goodbyes somehow made the place feel bleaker than I'd imagined possible.

Gran pointed to a plump, many pierced young woman dressed in unflattering black Lycra from head to toe and said, "Sugar me, it's her again, I know her. It's... er, it's Thingy Wotsit, the weddin' and funeral singer. She gets around does that one. Her mum ought to buy her a mirror, it'd be a kindness to us all."

I shook my head, avoided all eye contact and swiftly guided my sweet granny to sit on a nearby pew.

The Crem's duty vicar began the service by introducing Thingy Wotsit as John's niece, Alice, who then proceeded to sing Amazing Grace a cappella and slightly off-key. Gran covered her ears while I looked around for Alice's Uncle - I couldn't find him. I took hold of Gran's right hand and leaning in close asked, "Where's your neighbour?"

"In the box," she replied loudly, drawing stares of disapproval.

"Ssh, Gran, keep your voice down. I meant, where's the singer's uncle?"

"Are you deaf?" she asked in a ludicrously loud stage whisper.

"No, Gran. Can you see John, your neighbour who loves curry? His wife was Punjabi, a brilliant cook. He should be experiencing this recital with the rest of us."

"Ssh, Susan, listen to the lovely song, one of us ought to have the pleasure."

"When I'm old and crazy like you, Gran, I hope they shoot me."

Alice Thingy Wotsit chose the precise moment those words left my mouth to stop crucifying the hymn, which somehow created the impression that I was shouting at my daft old bat of a grandmother. The pompous vicar glared at me in a most unforgiving manner while he said, "Thank you Alice, now let us remember the solemn reason we are gathered here today..."

My phone vibrated in my pocket, I snatched it out and saw caller display warning me that it was the Boss in a Million desiring my attention. Gran added her glare to the vicar's. I muttered, "Good God, it's the bloody, bastarding control freak," then I crossed myself and practically sprinted out of the chapel.

I answered the summons in the stone flagged porch where I stood sheltering from the downpour with the hearse driver, breathing in his cigarette smoke and the cloying scent of half-a-dozen sad looking wreaths.

Ending the call with two fawning 'sorrys' and three groveling 'right-aways,' I decided to skip the rest of the service and wait for Gran to hobble out. My guardian angel must have been looking after me because, at the exact moment the driver (a man clearly unused to female company) got an unsolicited glint in his eye, the rain stopped and I spotted Alice's Uncle John resting on a nearby bench. Given my location and earlier blasphemy I gave thanks to God, unglued myself from the driver's goosebump provoking stares and made my way over to John for a chat with someone normal.

Sitting beside him on the wet seat, I elbowed him in the ribs and teased, "Hey, John, shouldn't you be inside with the rest of the coffin-dodgers?"

"I am." He replied, his voice gentle as the breeze.

"Right you are, I understand perfectly; you're there in spirit just like me. I bloody hate funerals."

John nodded and said, "They aren't a lot of fun. Even when the deceased's life was no fairytale..."

I interrupted him saying, "No princess, no talking animals, no happily ever after…"

John raised an eyebrow and said, "Well yes, even after such an ordinary life I can't bear to watch when the coffin rolls behind those awful red velvet curtains and you know the poor sod is on the way to a final barbeque."

He looked so sad that I wanted to hug him. Then he gave me a small smile and said, "The funeral is over now. Please remember to tell your lovely gran goodbye from me, I tried to tell her myself just before you collected her, but she wasn't listening."

I laughed and said, "She never is, John. Thanks for your company; you saved me from a pervert in a bad suit. Bye."

I left him on the bench admiring a rainbow and wondered how soon I could get back to the office; I didn't fancy making too much time up for a duty call.

Gran was waiting for me in the porch, leaning on her stick, flirting with the disappointed driver and admiring the damp floral tributes. I took her arm and in my chirpiest voice said, "Come along, my lady, your royal carriage awaits and my charming boss is desperate to see me, so let's be off."

After going through the same strapping in ceremony followed by another dare-devil ride among traffic jams I delivered my unusually quiet grandmother home. Back in her tiny apartment, I settled her into her over stuffed armchair, threw my expensive brolly in the waste, pinched another biscuit and prepared to make my excuses for an obedient dash back to the office. Then it occurred to me that I'd never bothered to ask the polite and obvious question, so I said, "Gran, I'm sorry, I should have asked before the service – whose funeral was that?"

Was that a tear in her eye? I stared, horrified as it rolled down her cheek filling her wrinkles like a flash flood. I pulled a hardly used soggy tissue out of my pocket and my gran, a woman I had never before seen show a moment's weakness, dabbed at her eyes sniffling as she said, "I thought you knew." I shook my head. "No? Oh Sue, it was John's funeral, y'know John, his wife was Punjabi. He was such a good friend to me despite stinking of that foreign muck. I shall miss him so much."

Before my knees gave way I slumped into the chair opposite her. Gran blew her nose and said, "Sue, are you OK? You look like you've seen a ghost."

"I think I have. I saw John twice today, first here when I came to collect you and then during the funeral. I spoke with him in the crematorium garden. He asked me to tell you he said goodbye."

Gran's teary eyes shone with excitement as she said. "I always hoped you'd inherit my gift. This is great news. I know what we can do, you ring your boss and tell him to stick his job. I'll put the kettle on for a nice cup of tea then and we can have a chat about your future career in spiritualism or, as I like to call it, spookerology."

The End

About the Author: Leo Kane

Over the years, Leo's experiences with people from all walks of life and cultures created a compelling curiosity with the darker side of the human psyche. So, ten years ago, Leo qualified as a Clinical Hypnotherapist specialising in the satisfying task of curing people of their fears and phobias. As you might expect a few of the more disturbed clients wandered into Leo's imagination and now find themselves in *Heavensgate*.

In 2008, Leo resigned her position as a Strategic Director in one of the UK's largest local authorities along with her judiciary role in the Employment Tribunal. She and her husband, David, took the decision to emigrate to warmer climes where, free of the day jobs, Leo's ambition to become a writer could finally begin to take shape. This major life change was both terrifying and exhilarating and, for the next few years, all consuming and from a literary success point of view, utterly pointless.

Books by Leo Kane:
Heavensgate: Hope
Heavensgate: Joy

Links:
Website: http://hgleokane.wix.com/heavensgate

Jericho Jordan

By Natalie J Case

From her earliest memory, she knew that there were no such things as fairy-tales, not for her anyway. Jericho Jordan was unwanted by the people around her. Worse than that, she was different. It was written in her red-brown skin, in the freckles that crawled across her wide nose, in the thick head of wiry black hair that resisted all urge to be tamed, and in the odd, pale green of her eyes.

She shaded those eyes and squinted into the late afternoon glare of the hot sun bouncing off the red rocks. Dust rose in the distance, vehicles of some sort dragging through the desert that separated them from the rest of civilization, toward the scattering of small towns that grew up out of the rock as the desert gave way to mountain and mines.

They didn't get many visitors and those that came never really stayed.

She tore her eyes from the line of vehicles, at least three that she could make out, and looked down at the town where she had been raised. It wasn't much. Most of the homes were built down into the rock in an effort to escape the heat, with just vents and heat releases visible above ground. There were some buildings, mostly ancient structures that had survived from before, gutted and repurposed to serve as meeting space and church, a school and other com-munity buildings. All told there weren't a hundred people living in the very loosely defined town.

On the west side was the mountain, the yawning opening of the mine where men and women disappeared every day and came out later with metals that sold on the other side of the desert to buy the things they couldn't grow or make themselves. The range stretched out into the north, cutting through the desert and up into where there had once been a forest.

To the south was the wall, a defense that only served to keep at bay the reminder of how the world had ended. The wall had crumbled in places, and there were ways over and through it if you knew how to look. The town of Judah gave way to desert in the north and east, red and black sands and dry brown weeds as far as the eye could see. The south though, beyond the wall was a playground of ruins and relics from before, abandoned and forbidden. It lay between the now and then of the world, cutting a line from the mountain out to the ocean, or so they were told by the elders. The badlands were off limits, the place of boogie men and history that had long since been rewritten.

Jericho dropped off that wall, her arm on the worn leather satchel over her shoulder to keep it from falling. She was late and she knew it. She knew it meant getting screamed at and assigned extra chores, but it beat spending the long, hot afternoon hiding from the heat and Mother Ruth in one of her worse moods. Of course, getting caught coming over the wall would earn her far more than extra chores.

She picked her way over the rocky terrain, her eyes skipping up to check the progress of the coming vehicles. She could tell they were black, big. They were land skimmers, the kind only the very wealthy could afford. They seemed to have turned west and north, so they weren't coming near enough to learn more. She shook her head and told herself she had to be wrong. No one wealthy ever came out to the wall.

Before she even made the turn that would take her up the dry creek bed, bringing her to what passed as her home, she could tell Mother Ruth was not happy. The whole area seemed to vibrate with anger and the Jericho could not escape the emotion as it sank into her. That too was another reason she was so despised. She did her best to hide it, but she knew things she shouldn't and that was a problem here in Judah.

Jericho slipped up to the back of the house, pausing to move one of the rocks that lined the small amount of building that cleared the ground. She had created a space beneath the stone, a place of her own to hide things that Mother Ruth would only take away from her. She stuffed the satchel into the space and eased the stone back down before turning to the back door.

"You better get in there."

Jericho looked up at the pale face of the youngest boy currently living under Mother Ruth's graces. "Yeah, what's got her twisted up now, Dex?"

He shrugged like it didn't really matter, but she knew better. Like her, Dex was unwanted...the product of an unwed mother, damned from birth. At least he fit in physically, his hair and eyes the right shade, his skin properly peach that deepened to a soft tan in the sun.

"Petre saw you go over the wall."

"Shit." She hesitated, eyeing the distance back to the wall and considering just grabbing her bag and running, but she wasn't prepared for more than an afternoon rummaging the ruins. She'd need food and water and...she drew a deep breath and squared her shoulders. It wouldn't be the first beating she'd endured, and it probably wouldn't be her last. "Thanks for letting me know. Get scarce, I don't want any of it blowing back on you."

She tucked loose strands of hair behind her ears and adjusted the tightly plaited braids that was her attempt at keeping her unruly hair from being offensive, while Dex wandered off toward the dirt road that connected the dwellings together. She headed down the steps and in through the back door into the kitchen. Sara sneered at her from where she stood cooking. "Mama! She's back!"

"Thanks for that." Jericho said snidely.

"You're going to get it."

Jericho took two steps toward the doorway into the rest of the house, figuring it would be easier to just face her fate, but she didn't have to go far. A hand grabbed her by the braid and physically dragged her into the main room, where the family sat to eat or to watch someone being punished, usually her.

Of course, family was a vague term. Mother Ruth was sort of the town's matriarch, keeper of wayward children and foster mother to those who were orphaned or abandoned. Of the five kids currently living there, the only one with any direct relation to Mother Ruth was Sara, who was the daughter of Ruth's only son, who had died when Sara was small. Dex was likely a distant cousin, and Levi and Matthew were brothers who had been found nearly dead in a beat up trailer beside their dead parents when they were only one and two years old.

Ruth was a woman well into her sixties, but she was strong with a heavy hand and a sense of religious morality that she felt it was her duty to impart by any means necessary to those in her charge. She dragged Jericho into the room and over to the punishment corner, shoving her head at the wall and commanding that she strip.

Jericho knew how this would play out and while instinct drove her to rebel, she simply dropped her light jacket and unbuttoned her shirt, dropping it to her feet as well. She pulled her pants down, leaving her standing slightly bent over in nothing but her undergarments. The rage was nearly palpable, Jericho could feet it in her stomach, even though Mother Ruth hadn't said a word yet. This wasn't going to be a spanking. This would leave marks.

"Levi, bring me the cane."

Jericho bit her tongue and didn't say a word. The first touch of the thin bamboo cane made her gasp, but she forced herself to be quiet as the cane came down over her ass. Even through the cloth of her undergarment, the blows hurt, but they were nothing compared to the first blow against flesh. She fought to keep from making noise, but lost the battle as the cane rained down on her back over and over again.

Her knees began to tremble as sweat trickled down her back and they buckled completely with the final blow. Ruth's hand was still in her hair and she squatted next to Jericho as she gulped in air and tried not to cry from the pain.

"You are lucky I don't throw you over that wall and leave you to die in hell where you belong." Ruth said fiercely into her ear. "I'm done being kind to you, devil-spawn. From this moment on I will treat you like the demon you are."

Jericho quivered as Ruth made her words abundantly clear, holding out her hand and bringing it back with a rusty metal manacle. She fitted it to Jericho's neck, tight enough that it would keep her to minimal head movement. It sat hot and heavy, thick against the column of her neck.

Behind her, one of the boys was laughing. Her back screamed in pain and her humiliation wasn't over yet. Ruth shoved her so that she was kneeling up, lifting each of her braids in turn and cutting them off with the kitchen shears Sara handed her.

Ruth dragged her then, her fingers twisted in what was left of Jericho's hair, out of the common room and down a flight of stairs and into the closet that served as the place she put Jericho to think about what she'd done. Ruth pushed her in, then leaned in around her to attach a chain to the heavy manacle, further limiting her movement.

"You will learn your place or you will burn in the fires of the righteous wrath of God." Ruth said furiously. "Three days in the closet and you'll do all the chores yourself for two weeks."

* * *

It was difficult to determine time in the closet. There was no food, no light. Just Jericho, the chains and the sound of Mother Ruth's voice reading from the book of law that came intermittently through a speaker mounted somewhere above her.

With the manacle around her neck chained to the wall, she was forced to remain on her knees, even when she dozed off.

Her back burned, from her neck down to her thighs and at least a few of the welts had broken open at some point. Jericho shifted and tried to find a more comfortable position, but Mother Ruth had made certain there wasn't one.

About the only movement allowed to her was the raising of her arms, but that made the welts on her back stretch and break open. She found herself drifting in semi-consciousness, some part of her repeating the endless litany of scripture that she had long since memorized from previous days spent in the closet. Her mind drifted, spurred by the sense of Ruth's rage that was as palpable to her as if it were her own, down the long corridor of memory.

She had not been born there in Judah. She and her mother had come from somewhere else, riding in a beat up quadwheel that broke down just outside of the town, or at least that's what she had been told. They were unwanted, outlanders, strangers. Jericho knew that she'd been barely days old when they were found, and that her mother had died just hours later.

But Judah was all she had ever really known.

Jericho started up from a daze as she heard voices, then the closet was opening and Ruth was there, unchaining her and pulling her backward, unlocking the manacle. There was a basin of water and clean clothes. Ruth handed her a glass of water. "Drink it. Clean yourself up. Get dressed and get upstairs. Best behavior, we got company."

She gulped the water down, uncertain how long she had been in the closet, and looked at the water basin. Impatient, Ruth pushed her, squeezing water out of a cloth and lifting it to wipe at the blood down Jericho's back. Jericho bit her tongue to quell the sounds of her discomfort and let Ruth do her work. When she was deemed clean enough, Ruth thrust the clothing at her.

"Go on then." Ruth turned on her heel and disappeared up the stairs, leaving Jericho to dress herself in the dress and stockings she usually only wore to temple gatherings. She dressed as quickly as she could, stretching aching muscles as she went. The dress was her least favorite piece of clothing, the material thick and stifling, an ugly brown that made her skin look oddly yellow. It was secured with buttons down the front, from her neck to her knee.

Ruth had left her temple shoes by the door to the stairs. Jericho slipped them on and ran a hand through what was left of her hair. It would grow out quickly enough, but in the meantime it would look exactly like Mother Ruth wanted it to, short and uneven and further display of her demon nature. She sighed and headed up the stairs before Ruth could decide she was taking too long.

The air felt different as she climbed the stairs. Ruth was still angry, but she was suppressing it. The others were all quiet, as if swallowing their emotion and stifled by... fear. Jericho recognized the emotion as she topped the stairs.

She had no idea who would be visiting them or why it would bring Ruth down to let her out of the punishment closet, but she was fairly certain that good clothes was a sign of something bad, and the dread and anxiety slipping down to meet her only added to her dread. She emerged at the top of the stairs and stepped through the hall, into the living space that was crowded with the kids Ruth cared for and four people in clothes that marked them from the city. Maybe even from off world.

The one woman among them smiled at Jericho as she came into the room, softening the hard look of her features. She tucked a strand of bright red hair behind an ear and glanced at Ruth in expectation.

"This is her." Ruth said, grabbing Jericho by the shoulder and thrusting her into the open space in the middle of the room.

"Jericho Jordan?" one of the men asked.

Jericho nodded. "Yes, sir." Her heart was racing. They were government people. Not Judah government, obviously. No one in Judah looked like them.

"How old are you, Jericho?" A different man spoke this time, the older one with the longer hair.

"Fifteen." Jericho answered. "Sixteen in a half cycle."

The woman nodded and opened a case she was holding, withdrawing an odd looking instrument. "Right age."

"Your adoptive mother here tells us that your birth mother died when you were young and that you came from somewhere outside of Judah," the long haired gentleman said.

"Yes, sir." Jericho confirmed. "I don't rightly know much. Mother Ruth only said they found me."

"Do you remember your mother?" the woman asked as she fiddled with the device in her hand. "Do you know her name?"

Jericho bit her lip. "No ma'am. She died from having me. I have a picture." Jericho glanced back at Ruth. She was supposed to have destroyed it. "Name on it says Malla."

The woman took a step forward. "Okay, Jericho, we need to draw a little bit of your blood. Hold out your hand."

Hesitantly, Jericho held out her right hand. The woman had a surprisingly strong grip and she used it to pull Jericho's hand closer before she brought the instrument down and pressed it against her finger. There was a quick prick and then the woman was drawing back. She fiddled with the instrument some more, then handed it to the only man who hadn't spoken.

He nodded once, then stepped around the others. "Jericho, my Jordan is Issac Manns. I have been looking for you for a very long time." He was guarded, his presence smooth, unruffled...all four of them were, so unlike the rest of the room.

Jericho could feel herself frowning. "Why?" Ruth was getting angry again. Jericho instinctively took a step closer to the man.

"You are a very special person, Jericho. Your mother was part of an experiment."

She frowned harder. "Experiment?"

He nodded. "Tell me, Jericho, do you have any special...abilities? Things you do that no one else can?"

Jericho bit her lip and inched another step out of Ruth's reach. "I feel things." She wasn't supposed to talk about it. Ruth had always told her it was evil, that she was being used by demons. "Things...like..."

"Watch yourself, girl." Ruth warned.

Jericho could feel the eyes of the others, all waiting for her to screw up, for her to speak, to say the wrong thing. The woman stepped closer, sliding an arm around Jericho's shoulders, making her stiffen and hiss as the heat of her seeped through the dress and the weight of her arm pressed against wounds that were still raw. Jericho felt a flash of concern and the woman pulled her arm away just enough that it didn't cause her pain.

In a very low voice, she said, "I won't let her hurt you. It's okay."

Jericho swallowed. "I can feel what other people feel. Emotions, physical pain."

The oldest man smiled. "Very good."

"We want you to come with us." The woman's hand slid down Jericho's arm.

"Come with you?" Jericho asked. "Away from Judah?" She glanced aside at Ruth and licked her lips. Maybe this was it, her fairytale moment. Like that girl in that story she'd read over the wall, only these people weren't some prince come to sweep her off her feet.

"Away from Judah," the woman confirmed. "There is a place where we can help you, teach you."

"For good?" Jericho asked, daring to hope for the first time that maybe she'd found a way out of her own personal hell.

"If you leave here, you won't be welcome back." Ruth said, her voice menacing.

Jericho already knew she would leave with them. She'd known it almost immediately. There was nothing keeping her in Judah. She nodded. "I'll go. I have no need of ever coming back here." She turned, scanning the room until she found Dex, his heart racing and his eyes already filling with tears. She went to him, hugging him tightly. "Keep your head down and don't provoke her," she said into his ear.

She let go of him and turned away as quickly as she could, biting her tongue to keep herself calm. Ruth was staring at her, her rage filling the air as the four outlanders circled around Jericho and they headed out the door and up the stairs.

It was close to evening, the air still and stifling. Three land skimmers were waiting for them, their sleek black dulled by dust. The woman led Jericho to the middle vehicle, opening the door.

"Jericho!" Dex was yelling her name and she turned as he came running from near the back door, her leather satchel in his hands. "Jericho!" He came to a breathless halt and thrust the bag at her.

"Thanks." She kissed is cheek. "Watch your back."

He sort of smiled and nodded, backing away as the land skimmer's engines started.

Jericho swallowed a sudden sense of dread as she peered into the darkened vehicle. She'd never been in anything so fancy. Not that she could remember anyway. She climbed in, moving across the seat and setting her satchel at her feet. It wasn't quite as hot in the car. The woman got in beside her and closed the door.

Jericho almost didn't feel it as the skimmer moved, and she held onto the seat for the first few minutes, before turning her eyes to the dark window, watching the town slip away as they moved out into the desert.

"My Jordan is Nadine Dokchev. I'm going to help you through this."

Jericho looked at her. Now that they were out of the range of Ruth's fear and anger, Jericho could read a little more from her. She was younger than Jericho had first presumed, late twenties at the outside. Like Jericho, her skin was darker than the people of Judah and Jericho wasn't sure that her hair was a natural shade. There was a vague sense of satisfaction, a pleased sense of accomplishment coming from her.

"What exactly is this?" Jericho asked, watching her carefully. Her blue eyes skipped over Jericho, then down to the case on the seat between them. She pulled some sort of tablet from the case, the screen coming to life with the touch of her fingers.

"This is the start of your new life." Nadine said. "We're going to go into Liamont City where we will get a full medical exam so we can determine our course of action for your development."

"My development." Jericho repeated the words, not sure what was meant by them.

"From there, we will design a series of classes and experiences for you."

Jericho turned to look out the window, but there wasn't much to see. They had passed into the desert and the suns had both set beyond the distant horizon. She had a vague memory of another night time drive across this desert. She knew it wasn't her own memory. She'd never been outside the walled town. But if she closed her eyes she could almost taste the desperation and fear, and she knew she was running away from something. Or someone.

Jericho pushed it away, convinced it was her mind playing with things she'd heard and seen, remembering things from the stories she'd found over the wall, the rooms filled with books filling her head with nonsense. "So, this experiment you say my mother was part of..." Jericho looked at Nadine, trying to feel past the cool exterior she was projecting.

"You'll get all the details later. For now, I can tell you that it was part of a genetics experiment. The scientists involved were trying to isolate and improve certain genetic anomalies."

Jericho sat back against the cool leather of the seat, but it hurt pressed against the welts so she sat forward again. "Like what?"

Nadine set the tablet down on her lap and looked at her. "Like your empathy, for example. That's what it's called when you can feel what other people feel. It's a part of all human beings, on some level. It's how we relate to one another, why we can feel bad when someone else gets hurt. In some people, it's more pronounced."

"Why? I mean... why would anyone want to make it so that I can feel someone else's pain?"

"Because, Jericho, what you have can be so much more. Wait until we are done teaching you how to access it and use it."

"Use it for what?"

Nadine smiled and patted her knee. "The opportunities ahead of you are endless. Let's take it slow at first, okay? It's a long ride, go ahead and get comfortable." She lifted the tablet and clearly dismissed Jericho's presence.

She wasn't sure how she felt about what had just happened, about the fact that they wanted her because of what she could do, something she'd been taught to fear and hide. It wasn't salvation, she knew instinctively. She hadn't stepped out of hell and into a story with a happy ending.

All she knew was that anywhere had to be better than in Mother Ruth's hands.

The End

About the Author: Natalie J Case

An avid reader from a very early age, Natalie grew up in worlds that only exist in books. Her influences run the gamut of genres, from childhood mysteries like Nancy Drew and The Bobsey Twins to epic fantasy and hardcore sci-fi.

Jericho Jordan is an introduction to a character and story that will likely come to fruition sometime in 2018. Currently, she is working on the second series in the *Shades and Shadows* series, a set of paranormal thrillers. The first in that series, *Through Shade and Shadow* was released in 2017.

Books by Natalie J Case:
Forever
Through Shade and Shadow

Links:
Facebook: https://www.facebook.com/authornataliejcase/
Twitter: http://twitter.com/nataliejcase
Website: https://nataliejcase.com/

It All Comes Down

by J.W. Goodwin

On goes the uniform as another day rises. A dull roar of people can be heard from beyond the door causing pressure to build inside Danika's chest. The swish of the apron was a sign that her work attire was ready to be dirtied again. Her hand paused at the door handle. Once she opened the door there was no stopping the rush of people, the thought hastened her heartbeat. She rubbed her shoulder, painful from the morning's run in with a local thief. "Just do your job and go home, one day at a time girl," she thought. One day at a time, no matter how hard it is.

Danika's life was no fairytale. There was no prince, no talking animals, no happily ever after. If there ever was, she missed the boat on that one. All she ever had was heartbreak and stress yet all around her there was proof that the ending does exist. Each couple she'd see holding hands made her awareness of the bitterness of her lonesome life more apparent. She could blame many things but there was one she came back to time and again. Why did her author forget to add a prince for her?

A continuous beeping of the scanner was a lullaby, while grabbing the next food stuff and passing it on a conveyor belt was a useless exercise. There had to be more to life than mindless work, more than Danika's current existence. Spending days tossing packaged meals and fruits was not her first choice but bills needed to be paid. Bills she wouldn't have had had there been an opening in her field of study, one she was forced to choose by a high school 'counselor'. What a crock of donkey -

"Danika!" yelled out a burley woman from the second-floor balcony, "quit your daydreaming and hurry it up." Of course the supervisor would grump at her from across the room instead of approach her. That woman could never be bothered to clamber off her chair unless it made her look good and reliable. Danika missed the old supervisor, at least she helped out when they were swamped with people. Very much like her day was turning out to be.

The final hour of her shift couldn't have come fast enough. Danika's feet burned as she sat on a bus seat next to the window. Why couldn't they sit when they obviously remained in the same spot all day long? She had read up on it and it turned out many cultures allowed sitting at the cash for retail employees. If only she could work at one of those places then she wouldn't have to rub her feet every night to stave off the pain. If only she could be anywhere but there.

Music pumped through Danika's ear buds, downing out the city noise as she flicked up on her cellphone. Cruising though social media kept her claustrophobia at bay as well as kept her up to date with family and friends. She lived far away from them hoping for better job offers in the city. Boy was she ever wrong. She was so focused she hardly noticed when someone sat in the seat next to her. Driving wouldn't be as bad but it was too expensive. She had calculated that if she wanted a car she would have to give up her apartment. She would prefer the small, grungy living space she had to living out of a car.

The rain outside pounded on the windows cleaning them of dust. It was appropriate for the day she had. First Danika misplaced her keys only to find them on the floor near their usual spot. A new bill wormed its way into her mail box demanding more money that she couldn't spend. What it was for she couldn't figure out. A stranger tried to nab her purse while she waited for the morning bus resulting in a pulled shoulder and her being late. Coworkers picked on her again as they normally did, but their words cut deeper than they usual during lunch. Her current predicament was she didn't have an umbrella with her for protection.

It was always like that for her. Danika's life had turned into one mishap after another. School was great, she could stay by herself and study and was applauded for her work. Once that was over she had to go into society and she had no idea how to do that. Communication was never her strong suit and it was what she needed to survive. If only they taught her that at school instead of geography or algebra.

The weight of what her life had become pulled on her heart drawing out tears. How did it come to all that despair? What had she done wrong for her to fall so far? Danika's grades were good once she discovered her niche and had everything completed on time no matter the workload. She never rebelled beyond snitching an extra dessert now and then. Her parents were highly praised for her upbringing from many who crossed their path. All that preparation, work, and dedication was for nothing. She was worthless in the true world.

"Hey, uh… miss, are you ok?" The male voice intruded on her thoughts making her gasp. Danika hadn't realized that her playlist had ended. She looked over to her neighbor to find kindness in his calm blue eyes. There was nothing extraordinary about him. His brown hair was a bit of a mess as was his worn, grey hoodie with grease stained sleeves. His backpack had a zipper starting to fray and he held it on his lap. The one thing that stood out was a scar above his eyebrow.

His cheeks dusted with pink. "You wouldn't be the first to stare at it." Danika quickly turned away as her cheeks burned. How rude could she be? Not like she voluntarily talked to people that often, she preferred to keep to herself. "It's alright. I'm used to it now and it's been a great conversation piece." From the corner of her eye she saw the smirk flash on his lips for an instant. "But back to my question, are you alright? You were crying so…"

She balled her fists. Danika obviously disturbed the guy's commute to where ever he was going. A pressure built in her chest, one she had become familiar with. She took a deep breath in before letting it out slowly. "I'm fine. Sorry I bothered you." He looked to the backpack in his hands. She returned to the window, thankful the conversation was over.

The rain continued splattering on the window as the bus stopped to pick up more passengers. A crack of thunder made her jump and caused a child to cry. The mother tried to hush it but the child refused. Danika couldn't blame it. She didn't expect the storm to pick up as no weather reports stated so during her work shift. Not that they were right very often. She rubbed the palm of her hand while focusing on her breathing. She needed to calm down or else panic would set in. She feared another coming ever since the first trip to the hospital. She couldn't go there again.

A tap came to her shoulder. She jumped before looking over to see the young man wanted to talk again. She wanted to ignore him but couldn't, he had noticed her looking at him. She painfully removed one of her earbuds and waited.

He avoided her eyes and wringed his hands. "I've said that so much that I know when someone doesn't mean it. Life is hard I know but..." His head lowered and he didn't continue.

Danika played with the fabric on her purse. That man, that stranger, was the first to say something was off. No one had picked up on the turmoil inside as she learned to keep it hidden. All her friends and family hadn't visited in months which was a blessing. She could hear her father giving her a lecture and feel her mother's disappointment though her silence. Her few friends would tell her that she was over thinking it and that others had it worse. She should be able to fix everything on her own according to them and she came to expect it.

"If you want to talk about it we can get off at your stop and we can go to a coffee shop or something. Food helps me clear my head, gets foggy when you're hungry." Her stomach growled at the thought of food but she couldn't afford to get anything. It was another reason why she was glad no one visited. She couldn't imagine the scolding she would get if any of them found out about her empty fridge.

"I can't," Danika whispered. Tears pricked her eyes. She couldn't start crying again, not there. Not when someone was watching.

"It'll be my treat," he offered. "My mom says every lady deserves to be treated once in a while. I think it's been long overdue for you." More tears threatened to break the seal. Why now when she was so broken, so lost? Who was he to barge in on her life? "My name's Mike by the way."

"Why are you doing this? What do you want from me?" No one in that day and age was that kind without wanting something in return.

His eyebrows shot up high. "I don't want anything." Mike's eyes darted around to the other passengers. They paused when they met hers before widening. "I'm sorry I didn't want to upset you. I just..." Again, he dropped the subject and looked away.

Danika couldn't figure him out. She pegged him to be outgoing but the way he stopped mid-sentence caused red flags to go up for her. Maybe she should get off the bus earlier to see if he follows. If so she could call the police and be done with it. Then again, the rain was coming down hard, it would make for a long walk home if she was wrong and she couldn't risk getting sick. She needed all the hours she could get.

"I want to help you before you decide to take the same path I did." Mike mumbled as he wrung his oil stained hands. He rubbed his scar and winced at the touch. "That's why I offered taking you out for food." The way he talked she wondered if he had approached others before, like he was some sort of counselor. "I don't want to take advantage or harm you in anyway. I just want to talk."

Danika looked to her lap. A chance to talk to someone sounded nice, perhaps even needed. To talk to a complete stranger might not be the best idea but Mike suggested a public place. If anything were to go wrong she could seek help. She wiped the tears from her eyes. One change, she thought. One last try to make sense of everything that's gone wrong. If it doesn't help then she had only one option left. She hoped he had some insight she didn't.

"The only thing is I'm not sure if there's any places to eat around my place." She admitted, refusing to look at him. You would think for living there for over a year she would know of something.

"That's ok. I know this city like the back of my hand. Tell me the street and I'll think of something."

Mike's enthusiasm was contagious. A smile pulled at the corner of her lips, something she hadn't felt for a long time, at least not a genuine one. "I get off at the corner of Ferguson and Brown Street."

He let out a low whistle. "Not the nicest neighborhood you've chosen to live in but I do know of a place near there. Just don't expect some fancy cuisine."

Mike escorted Danika from the stop to a small cafe a few buildings away from her apartment complex. The door paint was faded and chipping away while one of the windows was boarded up due to broken glass. It was a normal sight for her block but knowing she was going inside caused her unease. Was she walking into a trap? She had to admit that going in there wasn't the smartest thing she'd ever agreed to.

Inside wasn't much better. The few booths in the cramped space were tattered and needed a good cleaning. A light over one of tables was broken and a spot on the wallpaper was torn. A glass display highlighted sweet treats beautifully decorated along with delectable sandwiches and was the highlight of the store. At the counter was a teenager looking at his phone, grumbling about something.

Mike approached the teen quietly and slammed his hands on the wooden counter. He gasped as he jumped from the stool he was sitting on. Eyes wide he stared at Mike before he snorted and returned to his phone. "Dad's out 'till later, come back then if he owes you something."

"You know that's no way to talk to customers Brad. Do I need to call Doug and tell him what kind of mess you've left?" The teen sat up, fully alert, shaking his head. "I didn't think so, besides I'm not here for the bill." Mike motioned towards Danika. "I'm here to eat with a friend unless you've stopped serving."

"Sign says open and dad wouldn't pay me if I turned you away." Brad stuck his phone in his pocket before pointing to the menu on the wall behind him. It was beautifully written in chalk with a few drawings scattered about. "Pick something and I'll get on it."

Danika looked over at the faded menu. Everything made her stomach growl and she knew that she couldn't pretend that what she'd been living off of was enough. What she couldn't give to have a true Thanksgiving dinner again with mashed potatoes, gravy, carrots and turkey. Her gaze dropped to the marked-up counter in front of her. She missed her family and wished she could visit them at least once but financial burdens prevented it. Memories of family gatherings filled her mind causing familiar pressure to build in her chest. She took a deep breath, she had to get her emotions under control. The cafe was no place to break down.

Her thoughts turned to her present situation. It wasn't right taking money from a stranger no matter how hungry she was. Perhaps she could get away with a glass of water and not be a burden to Mike. She was an adult and as such should be able to care for herself, even if her situation was dire. "Water only please," she mumbled.

"You can pick whatever you want, it's ok."

Danika shook her head. "I don't know you Mike, it wouldn't be right."

He crossed his arms and stared at her. Brad leaned forward seemingly taking and interest in the discussion. "What wouldn't be right is sending you home when you're hungry. You can't deny a growling stomach, I heard it." Mike reached out and put a hand on her shoulder. The touch was surprisingly comforting and was something she missed. Her father would do that when she had felt inadequate and it always calmed her fears. No other had that power, not until she met Mike. The memory made tears prick her eyes again. "Please pick something." She wiped her eyes with her hands and nodded, taking the hint that she wasn't getting away with nothing. They picked out their meals and took a seat in a booth.

Danika stirred the ice in her drink unsure of what to do. Mike had gone to wash up before eating, he had noticed his hands were still covered in grime from work. Her hands trembled as her mind wandered. How could a stranger know her thoughts? How come the only place she could afford to live was in a shady part of the city when she worked so hard? Why was she failing so miserable at adult life when school was so easy? Why did it all happen this way?

She held her head in her hands while trying to hold back tears. Her whole body trembled. Her breath short and quick. Why, oh why did she leave home? Why did she think she could do it on her own?

A strong hand squeezed her shoulder. Danika froze. Her father wasn't there, her parents were always busy with work or something. She had to control herself and remember she was in public. That was not the place to lose her emotions, she had to keep calm.

"Hey," Mike whispered gently kneeling beside her," it'll be ok, tell me what's bugging you. We'll figure it out." How she wished she had someone close to her as kind as him. How she wished someone could understand the pain coming from within. There was never such a person, not one.

She shook her head. "No one can help. I'm an adult. I can do this on my own, I have to."

"Well that's a load of bull." Mike sat across from her and pulled his sandwich closer. He took a bite and swallowed. "No one has done anything significant on their own. History shows things turn out better when we work together."

"Experience tells me a different story," she mumbled. How many group projects nearly failed due to people not chipping in? All the work she had to do on her own to make it pass while other people reap the benefits. How many relationships had she witnessed fail because people can't be faithful? How many of her own relationships broke apart because the other moved on? Everyone in the city and back in her hometown lived for themselves, not a one helped the other unless there was some benefit to them.

Mike sighed before taking another bite of his meal. He stared off at the old wallpaper while he devoured the sandwich. Danika took a bite of her own and was pleasantly surprised at the taste. She expected a poorly made sandwich but Brad obviously knew how to throw together a good ham and cheese.

The rain hammered away at the dirty window as the lights flickered inside. People in the apartments above stomped quickly to the other end of the building disturbing the dust on the ceiling. The dust floated down like sad, little snowflakes and she watched it with thoughts weighing heavily on her heart.

Her existence was a joke much like the particles that floated around her. There was no meaning to her life.

Mike finished eating by washing it all down with a glass of water. "Well now that I've got food in me I feel much better. How 'bout you?" Danika nodded, the nourishment did make her stomach more at ease but not her mind. He stretched before lacing his fingers behind his head and closed his eyes. A smile pulled at the scar on his eyebrow as he let out a deep breath.

"You feel up to talking now or did I push too hard?"

"I don't think you can help Mike, no matter how much I tell you, I'm sorry." Danika wrung her hands. She couldn't tell anyone what she wanted to do no matter how much they prodded. The entire idea was frowned upon but she needed to find a way out. Her body shook with each breath. She couldn't keep living how she was, it was killing her.

"Maybe not but I'd like to try."

Danika shook her head. "I'm not dragging anyone else into this." She stood, wanting to quit the conversation. She wanted to leave but a part of her wanted to stay. Maybe he could help but no, she couldn't let him in. She'd just hurt him when she decided to disappear. She had disappointed enough people in her life, she couldn't allow one more to fall prey to it.

Mike dug through his bag and took out a pen and paper. He quickly scribbled on it and handed it to her. "It's my cell number. If you ever want to chat about anything give me a call." Danika looked at the numbers before tears broke loose. He reached out and wiped one away with his thumb. The touch was so feather light she could have sworn it never happened. "Everything will be ok, trust me."

Danika turned and walked out of the cafe without saying a word. Once she closed the door, she ran as fast as she could through the rain. The large droplets jabbed her as they fell. She deserved each one for leaving a good man the way she did but he'd find someone better. Anyone else was better than her. Each prick of pain she earned for not living up to her potential.

She rushed through the security door of her building and flew up the stairs nearly knocking someone over on the way. She forced her key in the lock and yanked the door open. She went in and slammed it shut before sliding to the floor, leaving a streak of water. She couldn't hold it in anymore, all the emotion from meeting Mike and everything else that day burst out in loud, wailing tears as her body shook. A neighbor pounded on the wall calling out for her to hush but she couldn't, the pain was too great.

When the sobs eased Danika stood, leaning on the wall for support. It was time. She took lined paper and a pen from her dresser drawer and sat at the small table in her apartment. She stared at the blank papers knowing what she had to do but couldn't find the words to write.

Her phone buzzed from within her purse. She pulled it out and the message she saw broke her heart. Her mother was asking about her day as she always did before bed. She must have thought of her as a disappointment, there was no other explanation as to why she couldn't find another job. What kind of daughter moves away from home and never visits? Her brother always found time and money to go back and Danika's parents talked about him so fondly. They had their perfect child, they didn't need her.

Danika sent back her usual response of everything was fine and work was normal. If she mentioned she was treated for supper by a stranger her mother would call. She didn't want to talk to anyone after she had been crying. Her mother would worry and she couldn't have that happen. Her parents had enough on their plate.

Once her mother said her goodnight, she returned to the paper. Danika had to let them know it wasn't their fault, it was all hers. She was the useless one. She should have known better. It would not be right to leave them with questions. She picked up the pen and started on the task before her.

* * *

A few weeks had passed since Danika met Mike. She took him up on the offer to text him the next day when the supervisor was being particularly harsh. His reply made her smile though it was only an instant. Later the same evening she called him and chatted about different things. She loved the distraction and held onto the moment as long as she could. Once they hung up the darkness clung to her again.

A month later she was called into the manager's office before the start of her shift. That burly supervisor made a complaint that Danika had been harassing her at work. It was all lies of course, but one she couldn't fight against. Everyone knew that woman was the favorite out of all of them. Danika pleaded to keep her job, knowing she had done nothing wrong, but the manager quoted policy at her. At the end of the lecture she remained silent, there was nothing she could do to save the situation. The manager asked her to return the uniforms and not to bother returning. On her way out, she could see that monster sneer at her. What did she do to deserve such treatment?

Dull colors whizzed past the bus window. That was the end for her, without a job she couldn't afford a place to live. She doubted she could stretch her savings to cover the rent due in a week. There was no time to find something else, not like anyone would hire someone as useless as her. As she thought, she remembered her savings would barely fill a grocery bag with food. She would starve and be homeless.

The sky remained overcast as she reached a park. It was the first place she explored near her apartment when she moved in. Danika had hopes and dreams back then. She looked to the sky as she thought back to the first day. She had been so excited to make her mark on the world. She would find that perfect job and work hard to get promoted. She had everything planned out and knew exactly how to get what she wanted. Then her spirit was crushed by weeks of rejections and, with all her supposed talent, she could only find a grocer on the other end of town to work at.

She sat on a bench next to the rapids. She couldn't move back home, that was a failure. She couldn't go to a government agency for help, that was also failure. She couldn't ask to postpone the rent, that would never happen. As she had student loans, from a program she couldn't even use, she couldn't borrow money. There was nothing she could do. She was at the end.

She really was a failure. Nothing she did ever turned out right. Even when she had done nothing wrong and kept to herself like a good little girl, she still lost. The world was a nasty place and she had no reason to belong in it. Danika always knew that she couldn't fit in, even in school she was at odds with fellow students. She wished she never existed.

The hours crept by but Danika remained on the bench. Soon the sun had set and the only light was from the lamppost nearby. Less and less people passed before her, not a one turned to look. Was that all she was, part of the scenery? Was that all anyone was?

Danika decided to put her plan into action. She couldn't live with the hurt any longer. What was the point of trying, of forcing herself to get up every day when it all ended the same. Life tore her apart every second and it was nothing compared to broken bones or cuts. Physical pain can be cured and seen but mental sickness was different. No one could see it and, unless she talked to someone, no one would know. She refused to suffer further. She couldn't do it.

She walked over to the short stone wall that kept the public safe from the rushing waters below. She climbed and stood atop of it. The white flow felt inviting. She always loved water, even as a kid, and she thought it was a fitting end. She had tried cutting herself and a few other tactics but none of them worked. Each attempt she stopped because of some useless fear of pain. It had to be something with no turning back. Something she wasn't afraid of, like water.

Danika's toes touched the edge of the wall. All it took was a step forward. One step and all her pain would be gone. She would be free and she couldn't hurt anyone again. She couldn't be the disappointment she knew she had become. A lump rose in her chest as she thought about it. Her parents would be sad but only for a little while. Her brother's wife was expecting their first child and it was all her parents talked about. They looked forward to it. There was nothing so brilliant she could give to them. All she'd be is a lesson they'd warn the child about. Don't follow in your aunt's footsteps they'd say. Don't be such a waste like her they'd warn.

The rushing water was so enticing. One step. No! You can't. Yes, one step. Just one step. Tears flowed from her eyes. She could do this. It's just one step. One step Danika.

Someone yanked hard on her coat making her fall backwards. She cried out when she landed on the person. She swung her arm around and hit whoever pulled her with her elbow. They stopped her attack, making her fail again. She failed at the one thing that was supposed to be easy. Why couldn't she just die already!

Rough hands pulled her into an embrace. "What the hell are you doing Danika?" She froze. Mike had found her. Out of everyone it could have been, it was him. He had pulled her off. It was his fault she had to continue with the pain.

She forced herself out of his arms. "Why did you stop me? I wanted to jump. I don't want to be here anymore!"

"I know that. I've known that since I saw you on the bus that day." He ran his fingers through his hair. "That's why I wanted to talk to you. I could tell this was where you were headed." His eyes welled up with tears. "There's so much more than the pain Danika. I know it's all you see right now but it gets better."

"You know nothing of what I've been going through! Why can't you leave me alone?"

"I do know what it's like and that's why I can't let you do this. It's why I've got my scar." Mike sat on the stone wall and held his hands. "I was going through a difficult time. In school, I was picked on and even after I graduated for living in this part of town. Nothing ever went right for me. Even my girlfriend ran off with my best friend.

"I tried to hang myself in my parent's garage." He looked away from her and to the dirt below as his body shook. His knuckles were white as he gripped the wall. "The rope snapped and I hit my head off the workbench. My parents found me there in a pool of my own blood. The doctor said I was lucky to be alive but it certainly doesn't feel that way someday. Not when my memory is crap.

"I talked to you that day on the bus because you reminded me of myself during that time. You feel so lost, so alone, that no one would care if you're gone. It's not true." Mike moved and sat next to her on the ground and held her hand. "You parents will care, your siblings will care, your family and friends will care Danika. I will care."

She squeezed his hand. "But I can't do anything right. I've lost my job, I can't afford food or rent. I'm going to lose my apartment. If I go back home or get any help then I've failed. I can't fail when I've worked so hard. It's not fair that I've tried this hard to get nothing."

Mike rubbed her hand with his thumb. "That's not failure. Throwing away your life by jumping, that's failure. When you've hit bottom the only way to go is up, even if a little help is needed." He helped her from the ground but didn't let go of her hand. "I hate to do this but I gotta take you to the hospital. I can't have you throwing yourself off a wall again. I may not be around to catch you next time and I can't have that."

Danika followed him slowly. How was it that a stranger understood her so well? No that wasn't right. Mike wasn't a stranger, not any longer. He was the only one to be there when she needed someone there the most. Perhaps her destiny never had a prince and, for once, she could live with that. So long as her knight was right there beside her.

The End

About the Author: J.W. Goodwin

J.W. Goodwin is the author of the novel *By The Light of a Darkened Forest*. She was born and raised in Northern Ontario, Canada where she still resides. That is where her love of nature grew and her writing flourished. Even when she had moved away for a time in her heart she knew she would always return home.

Books by J. W. Goodwin:
By the Light of a Darkened Forest

Links:
Facebook: https://www.facebook.com/JessicaWGoodwin/
Twitter: https://twitter.com/JessWGoodwin

Cyber Space Fairy

By Mari Collier

"Well, look at who just floated in!" The Fairy Godmother sounded rather indignant. The Tooth Fairy, Nephele, the Blue Fairy, Ariel, and Lillie White looked up from their tea.

In the doorway of the Fairy Lounge hovered a multicolored fairy with red hair on one side of her head and purple on the other side. Tattoos ran down her arms and legs. A nose ring of silver adorned her light blue face, and little bolts of yellow shot off from her wings whenever she moved. The new arrival floated over to the older fairies, her bolts floating harmlessly upward.

The others tried to hide their inward shuddering. The Cyber Space Fairy had been such an adorable multi-colored sprite just forty-odd years ago. How could she change so?

"Hello, Cyber Space," the Fairy Godmother smiled. "And where have you been?"

The yellow eyes looked at her. "Why in Cyber Space, where else would one want to be?"

The Tooth Fairy smiled at her. "Why in a child's bedroom, seeing their angelic faces, and leaving a nice crisp dollar bill. Just knowing how happy they will be is heartwarming."

The Cyber Space Fairy laughed. "Oh, that is so silly. Most of the time the parents have left far more than a dollar. You even have a real problem finding them asleep so you can return before break of day, plus in today's world a dollar won't even buy a sack of candy, let alone the electronic equipment they are already playing with when they are awake and losing their baby teeth. Admit it, gaining access to their domain is difficult when they are still awake playing games or sending text messages. What do you do? Just toss the bill in their direction and say you delivered it?"

Fairy Godmother gasped. "Really, you don't need to insult your elders. We all perform important needed tasks. Just because you had a failure or two doesn't give you any right to be so snide and cast aspirations at others."

"What failures? My net is up and working seamlessly."

"Oh, I heard from one of my clients and she cannot find her web domain and part of the connection to another site seems to be missing. Then there was an entire group of people without internet service in the Los Angeles area that I read about in Fairy News. I could go on, but you see what I mean."

Nephele, the created cloud daughter of Zeus, snorted. She was so upset she changed from blue back into the color of the cloud Zeus used to create her. She shook and returned to the color of the sky. The blue didn't clash with light blue of the Blue Fairy sitting next to her. Then Wee Willie Winkie arrived in a grey-white sleeper, carrying his candle. He crawled up onto the sofa, blew out the candle, and stuck his thumb in his mouth before closing his eyes.

The Storm Fairy arrived in her customary flash of lightning. Bolts shot out from her wings and lodged in the ceiling. Black clouds surrounded her and then rearranged into a long, slinky black dress. "Hello, dahlings, having a bit of tea are we?" She winked as she sat in the remaining empty chair.

Nephele shifted in her seat as her left side seemed ready to float away. She used her wing to bat it back and it aligned itself into the proper body shape again. At least Wee Willie and Stormy had interrupted Cyber's rude speech.

Cyber, however, glared at Stormy for daring to interrupt. "In fact, none of you perform the useful tasks that I do. How many young, handsome Prince Charmings are there left in the world, Fairy Godmother? There are maybe one or two, but their security is so tight you'd never be able to get an unknown into a ball where they are. I've heard they do not attend such events. Horses wouldn't be allowed on the streets, and who goes home at midnight in a coach drawn by horses anyway? As for nobility, that is a laugh. They might exist, but for the most part they are just aging figure heads."

Stormy raised her eyebrow, and her cup filled with tea floated over. "Cyber, why would you pick on Fairy Godmother like that? She is in her dotage you know."

"Dotage? How dare you!" The Fairy God Mother stood. "Just because you have been raising havoc with your tornadoes, flooding and snowstorms, you think you can insult us that do good works?" She turned, flew to the door, and swirled around to announce, "I shall return when the company returns to normal."

With those words, she flew to the anteroom. Now what could she do for some poor wench that couldn't afford a ball. She sighed. Maybe there was a high school student somewhere that needed a Fairy Godmother to make her teenage dreams come true. Fairy Godmother left the building behind and flew off to begin her search. It had been a long time since she created a coach drawn by four matched horses. She wondered how many mice would be in a normal household now.

The others watched her leave and Cyber was smiling. "You see, she can't stand the truth. Thanks, Stormy. It's good to see you again."

Stormy's dark hair shook and her scarlet lips smiled. "You look like you've been busy, Cyber Space. What is it with all those tats?"

"Oh, these?" Cyber held out her arms. "They are such fun to have. See how I can change them." The tattoos of blue and green swirls became red and green dragons, the circles and animals on the other arm rearranged their position.

"As for what I have been doing, there is a new force on the net and information highway. I can now move what people say, do, and watch to where it is broken down into advertising data to be shared with the providers who pay for more and more cyber ware and faster access. That helps to create even more room on cyberspace."

Nephele looked at Cyber Space as though she were a mad child. "And how is that useful?"

"It makes the people happy to be so connected and the companies richer. As they build bigger and bigger data banks it makes me more powerful. I'm not like you old, useless fairies that really have nothing to do anymore. Stormy is the only other one that has driven or ridden more powerful forces across the world."

"What happens when that new force you spoke about becomes even more powerful? Does that leave room for you? By the way, what is this new force? Does it have wings?"

Cyber Space laughed. "You really don't know anything about the world out there, do you? We are all so connected and interdependent now. People are able to fly through the air in machines they have created and be in another country within hours. When they wage war, one weapon kills hundreds or more. So much for the striking power of the old gods, like your old man, Zeus. Transporting themselves or their favorites to other places or killing one mortal or semi-mortal with one bolt just doesn't cut it."

Nephele gasped. "That is blasphemy!" Her outrage was so great her body began to disintegrate. The Tooth Fairy and Lillie White both wrapped their arms around her to hold her together.

"Now look what you've done!" The Tooth Fairy was shouting. "How can you be so cruel to our oldest and dearest member?"

Cyber Space shrugged her shoulders. "Just name one reason why she exists. At least Lillie White Fairy can predict when Spring will happen, but since she can't talk no one really knows when it will happen, and so humans look at a stupid ground hog and pay no attention to a silent fairy fluttering about in the air. Which when you think about it, they can't see her either. She needs a tablet to post her petals online."

"You need to quit criticizing. The world of fairies includes you," snapped the Tooth Fairy. "It seems to me, Stormy is the only one humans as a group pay attention to any more. At least there are some children that still wait for me."

Cyber Space stood. "You are so wrong! Humans do pay attention to me. Who do you really think is Siri or Echo? It certainly isn't the Echo of fairy tales and myths. As for you, Tooth Fairy, when was the last time a child was excited about you or tried to stay awake long enough to see you? You can't name anyone, can you?"

Silence filled the room. "You see, you are all totally useless except for Stormy." She waved at them and flew to the door. "Ta, ta, darlings, but I must be off. The Net is calling me."

"Well," sputtered Nephene, "she was obnoxious as a child, but she has taken it to new heights!"

Cyber smiled with satisfaction as she lifted upward and caught the first electrical current. It carried her deep into the world of game avenues, videos streaming across space, and the messages crossing and crisscrossing the world. It was exciting and she summersaulted across the landscape when flashes of light interrupted her journey.

She used her wings to soar higher and surveyed the gray landscape to locate where the flashes came from. Was it something that required her expertise to keep the net flowing? Then she saw them, two rangy male fairies battling for a site.

The Malware Fairy was dressed in blue-black, his broad, black wings were soundless as they whipped the air and he moved sideways, up and down, twirling, and throwing his bolts at the red and deep blue Trojan Fairy.

Cyber sent her own bolt of electric particles flowing through the space between them. "Stop, you are forbidden in my world," she screamed.

The two male fairies emerged singed, but upright, and both turned towards Cyber to aim their next bolts at her. Before they could let loose, Cyber unleashed another blast that tossed them upward and then down. Both landed on their knees, flailing their wings to be upright, and Cyber flew upward to unleash the killing throw. She did not notice Nephene appearing behind her or see the electric bolt that hit her back, burning away her wings. She tried to stand, but another blast from Nephene sent her rolling over and over, spooling through the spaces she once ruled.

Nephene nodded and turned towards Malware and Trojan. Malware had regained his wing power and was about to send another bolt into the struggling to rise Trojan when Nephene's next bolt cut him in half and he smoldered away into blackness.

Trojan managed to fly upward, his wings gaining strength, the power surging through him again. He turned towards Nephene and held out his arms to her. "Mother, are you all right?"

Nephene fluttered over, her wings barely moving. "This space is so hard to move in, but I knew you would be in danger, my son." She patted his face with her wings and fell into his embrace.

"It's dangerous for you to be here, Mother."

"Oh, nonsense, my boy. I was at Troy too, if you will remember." She sighed. "That was so long ago."

"Who was that fairy that interrupted my battle?"

"She was a most annoying chit that had no manners. She needed a good lesson, but, you, my son, you really need to find a good war to fight. This space is so different."

"A war like at Troy doesn't exist anymore, Mother. The human battlefields of today have such powerful explosions they can blow one's wings away. Here is where I can annoy humans and fight against a common enemy, the Malware clan." He gave her one last hug, smiled at her, lifted his sword, and flew off into the blue-black space crisscrossed by silver and golden lines.

"Goodbye, my darling boy," Nephene cried after him and tried to work her wings enough to leave. The cyberspace closed around her. "Oh piffle," she snorted and snapped her fingers and disappeared from cyberspace. It was time for another cup of tea.

She floated back into the Tea Room. The Fairy God Mother had returned and was weeping into her cup. Lillie White Fairy was patting her on the arm. Stormy was sitting there smirking at them. They all looked at Nephene as she floated in and settled into a chair. The teapot floated over with a cup and saucer trailing.

Nephene watched as the tea poured into her cup. When it was the proper level, she added the creamy dew of clouds and fairy dust before taking a sip and then smiling at the rest.

"Welcome back," said Stormy. "I wasn't sure you could make a jaunt any-where. You're fortunate that Cyber isn't here to make you come apart again."

"Oh, we won't need to worry about her nasty remarks anymore." Nephene turned to the Fairy God Mother.

"Did you find someone to clothe and equip for a party or a prom?"

The Fairy Godmother looked up and wailed, "All she wanted was the glass slippers. She said my dress was dorky and screeched when she saw the mice. Then she ran out of the room without the glass slippers." Tears continued to roll down her face. "What is it with these modern young females that they can't even stand the sight of a mouse? Are they that incapable? Cindy had no such qualms." She took a drink of tea and dabbed at her eyes. "Cindy is Cinderella, you know."

"You have been trading on that one well known success fable for years," Stormy's words were scorn laced. "You need a new venue."

"Really, Stormy, must you pick on her?" The Tooth Fairy was frowning. "We are just enjoying ourselves. We don't need the jabs from your tongue. Your storms are bad enough."

"It's the new order of things, didn't you know? You really need to enter the current century or you will be falling apart like Nephene." She pointed at the half-way off the back left wing.

Lillie jumped up and returned the wing to its proper position and left a stream of flower petals between her chair and Nephene's.

"Oh, look, spring is almost here," said the Tooth Fairy. Lillie is predicting its arrival with her flower petals."

"See," snorted Stormy. "The same old scenario over and over. Maybe Cyber Fairy was right. White Fairy needs a tablet to let the world know that spring is coming. She could do a YouTube video. Maybe Cyber could give her some pointers. Right now her predictions are useless."

Collected gasps came from everyone but Nephele. She pointed a finger at Stormy and said, "Cyber won't be helping anyone. You had best hold your tongue or you'll be as useless as she is."

Stormy looked at Nephele. "What? You won't say that when she returns."

"Nephele, what have you done?" cried the Fairy Godmother. She was well aware of the powers the Hera look-a-like possessed.

"Let's just say that for Cyber Space Fairy there isn't a Prince Charming, there arem't any talking animals in cyberspace, and there's no happily ever after. She will just spool on forever."

The End

About the Author: Mari Collier

Mari Collier was born and raised on a farm in Iowa. From there she moved to Phoenix, then to North Bend, WA. When she retired, she found refuge in a small community in the high desert of California. She is an active member of the Twentynine Palms Historical Society and is on their Board of Directors. She writes two columns for the Old Schoolhouse Journal and enjoys family, friends, the local art galleries, and theaters.

Books by Mari Collier:
Earthbound
Gather The Children
Before We Leave
Return of the Maca
Thalia and Earth
Fall and Rise of the Macas
Twisted Tales from the Northwest
Twisted Tales from the Universe
Twisted Tales from the Desert
Twisted Tales from a Skewed Mind
Man, True Man
Links:
Facebook:
https://www.facebook.com/Mari-Collier-205325882886976/
Twitter: https://twitter.com/child7mari
Website: http://maricollier.com/

The Ginger Man

By Chris Tetreault-Blay

Declan Starker pushed his foot down a little harder on the accelerator, mindful of not letting his speed creep high enough that his wife Grace would notice that he was doing several miles over the limit. They were running late. He knew they would be. It happened every time.

He glanced in the rear view mirror and watched his little girl sleep, just for a second. It brought a smile to his face. She always exuded peace whenever she slept, calming him. Grace looked into the back of the car at the same moment, the proud parents sharing a momentary smile as Declan returned his gaze to the road ahead.

It was mid-morning, the sun now high above the trees and spraying its warmth through the windshield. Beads of sweat formed on Declan's brow, but not a reaction to the warmth of the day alone. His heart was racing and his body began to chill as he looked down at the clock on the dash. They were so late.

He had bundled his little family in the car in good time that morning, pleased that he had chosen to pack the cases and bags into the boot the night before. But the wretched road closure the wrong side of Axminster had forced them to take an unannounced detour through tight lanes. They got no further than half a mile through the village when the traffic stopped dead in front of them. The single-track lane was not designed to take that volume of traffic at one time, trying to force past each other in two directions.

Overall the diversion and subsequent jam had cost them nearly an hour. The race was now on to get to the ferry port, still some eighty-odd miles away and with only an hour and a half to get there. The only other thing he was thankful for, however, was that Eleanora had spent most of the journey asleep so far. Car journeys were always like a spin on the wheel of fortune – they could never predict just how many times they would have to stop for Ellie's impromptu toilet breaks, many of them false alarms.

But so far, so good. As soon as Declan was able to pull back onto the main road, he made up for lost time. They were now on the M27 bound for Portsmouth. The final stretch.

'It's sixty, love,' Grace informed him.

'No, we're on a motorway. National means seventy,' he replied brusquely but with a smile.

'Even so, you're doing eighty,' his wife replied. She always had to have the last word. It infuriated him only for a second, before he realised that he no longer had an argument.

'Haven't got time to hang around now thanks to them back there.' Declan had no idea what had caused the road closure, whether it was an accident that had ended in injury or fatality, but without the facts he decided that he was not obliged to care. It had been an inconvenience, and that was that.

Declan viewed the next marker board on the side of the motorway, trying to quickly calculate roughly how many minutes they had left to cover the rest of the miles. He had managed to pick up another five minutes, so decided that his speed had been justified. It was a small victory.

'I need a wee,' came the sweet monotone voice from the back of the car. Declan closed his eyes and squeezed the top of the steering wheel, frustrated once more. Grace looked at him, stifling a smile. Grace looked at him, stifling a smile. She always said he was doubly cute when he was stressed.

Grace turned in her seat and reached behind her, putting a hand on her daughter's leg. 'OK, sweetie. We will stop in a few minutes at the next services. Can you hold it for me?'

The little girl nodded, causing the dark curls that framed her cherub-like face to bounce. Grace glanced at her husband as she turned back around, placing a hand on his as it rested on the gear stick. Declan was bristling, and he knew that she could feel it too. 'It'll only be quick,' she said quietly, leaning towards him. 'I promise. We can't make her wait.'

Declan gave a single nod, looking once more into the rear-view mirror. Ellie smiled sweetly back at him, washing away the anger. He smiled back to her.

Within another mile, he followed the next exit towards the final service stop before Southampton.

* * *

The service stop didn't hold all of the luxuries of many. This one held merely a fuel station and a couple of large gravel car parks, with a sprawling playing field running behind. Without the luxury of an enclosed toilet, Grace bought the travel potty out of the backpack and set it on the ground next to the car. Declan sat at the wheel, the anxiety rising in him as he glanced at his watch every few seconds.

He heard one of the rear doors open again and looked back sharply. Grace lifted her eyebrows and shook her head with a smile as she grabbed the small knitted gingerbread man from Ellie's car seat. Despite all of the money that they had spent in her three years on countless toys, she never let go of the small cuddly toy that came free with her Christmas dress from a few months before.

A couple of minutes later, Grace buckled her daughter back into her car seat and Declan's hand turned the key even before his wife had settled into her seat.

'Ah bugger,' she said, 'I forgot to get rid of this.' She held up the used baggy from the travel potty and asked silently with her eyes for Declan to take it. He tutted as he took it and heaved himself from the car. He could feel their holiday steadily slipping away. He stood for a moment and swept his gaze around the car parks, noticing the single red metal bin at the far side of the car park. His feet crunched over the gravel as he stomped towards it. Within a few feet of the bin, he tossed the bag into the bin.

The rush of the speeding traffic from the motorway had masked the sudden commotion around where his car stood. It wasn't until he was on the other side of the hedge that separated the car parks that he saw the group of darkly-clad men that surrounded his car. Two steps closer and he heard Grace's cries.

With his final step, everything went black.

* * *

There were four of them. All dressed in black jeans and hooded tops. They had been in the empty kiosk shop when the Starker's had arrived. The leader of the group – the smallest of the lot – had been busy tying up the store clerk in the small store room out the back when one of the others had alerted him to their uninvited guests. Tightening the gag around the clerk's mouth and landing a fist heavily across his temple, the leader stomped to the front of the store and peered through the blinds on the door.

They waited, watching their every movement. The family were about to leave when suddenly they presented the villainous team with a fresh challenge; Declan left the car and took a stroll across the wide car parks, leaving his luscious wife alone.

Or so they thought.

There were no words, no questions ask and no answers given to what happened next. He led his band of minions out of the shop towards the car. Three of them surrounded each side of the vehicle as the Leader rushed to Grace's side and threw open the door. Grace, who had been oblivious to the group's arrival as she reached behind to tighten Ellie's harness, did not have time to scream as the Leader grabbed her hair and covered her mouth.

She was pulled from the car, her legs dragging across the gravel, the skin taken from her knees, before she was brought to her feet and then thrown onto her front across the bonnet of the car. The Leader stood behind her, commanding two of his minions to hold her in place as he loosened his belt and undid his fly.

'Bingo,' he said through his heavy breath. Grace was wearing a skirt, thus speeding up the process. One of the Leader's hands reached between her legs tore down her underwear and with one thrust he was inside her. She screamed. He howled in delight as he started to invade her body.

'No, please! Please!' Grace screamed. It did no good.

'Hey boss, we got company,' the third henchman called. As the tallest of the group, this man could clearly see over the car. Declan had started his return back to his family, but Grace's sudden scream had alerted him. He now started to move more quickly.

'Deal with him!' the Leader grunted.

The tall man left his post immediately and crossed behind the car, parallel to the path Declan was taking. A couple of strides later and he had crept up behind Declan. One of the tall man's gangly arms shot towards the sky, the iron bar in his fist glinting against the sun, before it was brought down against Declan's head. There was a sickening crunch as the blow broke his skull.

Declan fell limply to the ground, his body twitching. The tall man grabbed at the dying man's shirt collar and dragged his body through the dusty ground, dumping him next to the car.

'Easy!' he declared to the Leader upon his return. The Leader continued to pound away at Grace as he held up a fist towards the tall man, a gesture of their triumph. Grace's head was forced to look in the direction of her now dead husband, causing fresh screams. The sound of her struggle, of her horror, drove the Leader to the point of no return. With a few final gyrations, he groaned as his body tensed and began to shudder. Then his movements ceased, his face drawn in a sickly grin. His chest heaved as he tried to regain his breath.

'Finish her too,' he shouted towards the tall man, throwing Grace face-first to the ground. The tall man stepped towards her battered body and brought the bloodied bar down across her back, her shoulders, her head.

Three blows and it was all over, all in the time it took the Leader to secure the belt around his jeans once more.

The four men exchanged high fives, whooping with each slap. The two whose job had been to hold Grace across the bonnet walked around the car, cupping their eyes as they stared in through the windows, surveying their next getaway.

'Oh shit...' one of the smaller men said as he looked through the car window. 'Boss?' he yelled.

The Leader crossed to him, agitated, following the direction of the hench-man's finger as he pointed at the glass. He grabbed the handle and tore open the door to find Ellie, trembling violently in her seat. Her face now ashen, her tiny innocent eyes wide. She stared ahead towards the windscreen. Her breath shallowed, her nostrils flared with each attempt to suck in more air.

'Shit...' the Leader said as he stood frozen, a new form of reality now finding its place in his mind. His body ran cold as the child turned her head towards him.

Then she screamed. Indecipherable words spilled from her mouth as she fought to breathe, to speak. In one final act of cowardice, the group of darkly-clad men ran, leaving little Ellie to scream and sob to herself.

* * *

Even at only three-years-old, Ellie knew that everything she had just witnessed was wrong. She had no idea of what had truly just happened, only that it had caused her mummy pain. It had caused her to cry. These mean men, whoever they were, came out of nowhere and had grabbed her mummy, had hurt her, then thrown her to the ground.

She had witnessed the rape, saw her mother's terrified eyes and heard her muffled screams as she lay pinned to the front of the car. The shock quickly took hold, freezing her in her seat. She was trapped. Unable to breathe, unable to do anything.

Where was her daddy, too? Why had he left them and not returned? He would be back soon, she told herself.

As soon as the first scream left her body, it was like a dam had been broken. There was no stopping it. The world around her disappeared as she lost herself to the output of the terror she had been forced to witness.

She grew tired very quickly, but no-one came. Her cries soon dried up, leaving her chest sore and her eyes puffy. She sniffed, unable to make another sound. The hours passed and darkness descended. But nobody came.

The car door beside her had been left open, letting the chill of the evening air drift in and case itself around her. She started to shiver.

Ellie had never coped well with the dark. Her night light still had to be left on, for every time she woke she felt the shadows in her bedroom touching her. Now coupled with the cool night breeze, she felt them even more. She imagined long, dark bony fingers trailing over her.

Through it all, Ellie still had hold of the only thing that brought her comfort. The small, soft toy in her hand; her ginger-man. She squeezed it tighter, brought it to her face and hugged it close. Her tears soaked into his woollen body.

'Please don't leave me,' she sobbed. The new burst of tears lasted only a fraction of the time as before, before sleep took hold.

* * *

She didn't dream. It felt as though she only closed her eyes for a few moments, staring into the darkness, her mind finally numbed by the nothingness that it brought. But in truth, she lay asleep for over four hours as the night drew in. As her mind finally awoke, she thought she was at home on Christmas Day, gazing at the twinkling lights on the tinsel-laden tree.

But the colours grew and swirled before her, before they began to take form new shapes. Soon, her vision was filled with flashing shades of red and blue, against a black background. Whispers danced all around her, growing louder. The haze finally lifted as she prised her eyes open.

Ellie felt her body shake gently, but somehow knew that someone was shaking her.

'Sir, she's waking up!' shouted a woman. Ellie looked into the direction of the voice – just below where she still sat strapped into her car seat – and the policewoman's blonde cropper hair began to break through. The features of her face followed.

The little girl immediately panicked, shouted out for her mummy, her head thrashing side-to-side as she sought her parents. The friendly police officer touched her hands, calming her just a little. Then it all flooded back to her; the horror that she had been subjected to, the terrified look in the whites of her mother's eyes as she was abused and beaten by the cruel gang in black clothing.

Ellie screamed, her mouth unable to form any coherent words. Her parents had always been so proud of how her speech had come along considering Ellie's age. But at that moment, words failed her.

PC Julianna Selby reached for her, trying desperately to calm her down. The true shock was yet to set into the little girl's mind, and she needed to help keep her under control the best she could.

The scene had turned her stomach the moment she got out of the patrol car. The blood had not yet dried on the concrete, and still existed in thick smears on the ground, trickling to form neat pools around the front tyres of the car.

Both bodies lay face down. Their faces were largely untouched, but the vicious assaults had taken chunks out of their backs. Declan Starker's skull had been caved in from behind, his hair now matted with the dried blood and brain matter.

Thankfully, she had noticed the child in the back seat almost immediately, her discovery aided by the open rear door. She had found Ellie asleep, although for many frantic moments she thought her to be dead. Her skin was deathly pale, her skin ice cold. But as she knelt before her, she could hear her faint breathing.

Miss Selby had let her fellow officers clear up the mess behind her whilst she tried to gently rouse Ellie from her grief-stricken slumber. When it had finally worked, a rush of relief coursed through her, met only with fresh panic when

Ellie started thrashing out. She had to be careful to steady Ellie's heart rate, for there was no telling what damage had already been done to her on the inside. There was no physical sign of harm or struggle – at least the bastards who had butchered her parents had thought enough to spare her little life – Ellie's ordeal would have surely damaged her mind.

Selby looked over her shoulder towards her sergeant, silently asking for help or reassurance. It was only her second week with the force.

'Get her out of there,' the moustachioed chief shouted. Selby nodded, her hands wrestling with the buckles. As soon as the harness was released, she gently grabbed hold of the child and pulled her from the car. Ellie immediately wrapped herself around Selby, her legs circling her waist and her arms around her neck. Selby put a hand around and rested on one of Ellie's shoulders, quietly shushing her. Ellie's little body relaxed at last, as Selby carried her away from the carnage, taking care to keep her head pressed close against her so as not to catch a glimpse of her parents.

Selby carried her from the car park and sat her in the warmth of the awaiting patrol car, which waited in the nearby fuel station. As soon as Selby pulled away from her, Ellie began frantically searching her hands, her lap and her tiny pockets.

'What's the matter, dear?' Selby asked.

There was no answer; Ellie simply continued checking everywhere around her, growing more upset with each passing moment. Selby knelt before her, touched her hand and asked again. 'Slow down,' she told her, 'tell me what's wrong.'

'My ginger-man,' Ellie sniffed, still looking around, and even casting a look behind Selby, over her shoulder. 'My ginger-man,' she said again as a sob caught in her throat. 'He's gone!'

Selby got one of the other male officers to sit with Ellie as she returned to the car, trying to look for the child's lost toy but at the same time having no idea what she was looking for. At least he couldn't have gone far, Selby thought, since the child had not moved from her car seat. Selby returned to the car and checked the back seat.

Nothing.

She ducked down and searched the foot well below where Ellie had been sat, reaching under the front passengers' seat too.

Nothing.

She returned to the patrol car, dismissed the other officer and knelt down in front of Ellie once more and shook her head. 'I'm sorry, sweetie. I couldn't find him.' Ellie's body shook as she sobbed again, her cheeks and top lip now coated with a sheen of salty tears and snot. Selby reached for the little girl and held her close, whispering to her. 'I will find him, I promise.'

* * *

PC Selby took Ellie back to the station with her that night and made her a bed on the sofa in one of the consultation rooms. She sat in the corner of the room for the rest of the night, giving in to short dozes here and there but mostly just watching the child sleep. She tried to fathom what she must have seen, what would be left of her sanity in a few weeks when the shock and fatigue would have lifted and reality started to set in.

The next day, Ellie was moved to a safe-house; a large property near Stoney Cross, in the heart of the New Forest. Two nuns resided there, whose job it was to care for children of all ages that had been subjected to abuse, abandonment or loss. Children that just needed somewhere that sheltered them from harm. Crittenden Hall was largely unknown to the general public. The authorities kept it going, and maintained its secrecy, as it was a valuable resource for them. With the walls of the mansion, they could ensure that the most vulnerable of witnesses could be protected whilst they tried to find the perpetrators of whatever crime had robbed them of their innocence.

For weeks, Ellie did not sleep. Her eyes closed during the night, but she did not rest. Despite the constant company from the nuns and the other nine children currently in residence there, she felt alone. Even at such a young age, she felt betrayed by those around her.

She did not speak, but did not protest when the nuns moved her from her bedroom to the common room. She even joined in with the other children, playing with the abundance of toys at their disposal. But, as the Sisters observed, she would only seem at peace when playing alone, away from the others. They would watch her for almost an hour sometimes, marvelling at the depth of her imagination, wondering what scenes were going through her growing mind that were coming forth through her hands as she moved the dolls, plastic animals and dinosaurs around the carpet.

Sister Abigail, however, voiced concerns after the first month of Ellie's residence. In a sense, she was very much like the other children that passed through there. Her life was not a fairy tale. There was no prince, no talking animals. No happily ever after. But in many of the others, there, hidden beneath their grief - their fears - was hope. But there was something about Ellie. Something a lot more disconcerting.

One day, she had watched her in the play room as she played with a small army of Lego men. Her play was innocent enough to begin with, so Sister Abigail left her for a short while whilst she attended to two of the other older boys who were locked in a play wrestling match, one refusing to let the other out of a very tight headlock.

When she returned to Ellie, she was horrified to find all of the Lego men had been dismembered. Their heads, hands, arms, torsos and legs had all been removed from one another and now lie in neat piles. Ellie had by that point even moved on to lining the body parts up in their groups, arranging them by colour.

The sight was worrisome enough, but the sound emanating from Ellie's mouth was most disturbing of all. She was laughing. Quietly, and very deliberately, laughing.

'They won't misbehave anymore,' she told Sister Abigail without turning around to face her. Ellie's voice lacked tone, lacked any emotion at all.

As Sister Abigail took a step closer to observe the macabre display, she noticed a group of four yellow plastic men that had somehow escaped the torture of their friends. Their bodies remained intact, but piled upon each other as if kindling on a campfire.

'Wh-What about those ones?' Sister Abigail asked, pointed a crooked finger towards the small group of still-whole Lego men.

'They're next,' Ellie said coldly. 'They haven't found them yet.' With that, Ellie's head slowly turned to face the nun. Her eyes, which had previously been a warm autumnal brown, now shone an icy blue.

Sister Abigail brought a hand to her mouth as she trembled and stumbled backwards, out of the room. She ran down the hall, in search of her fellow sister, feeling the sudden need to hide.

* * *

Later that night, a call came through to Crittenden Hall. It was Sergeant Carter from the local police, requesting that he and one of his officers call round with some urgent news. Carter arrived at the house within the hour, with PC Selby at his side.

Sister Beatrice took them through to the main office, buried deep at the rear of the building. As they walked past the small bedrooms, PC Selby paused at one and looked in, seeing the familiar trail of thick dark curls above the pink duvet cover. Ellie lay on her side, her back to the door. She looked asleep, but somehow PC Selby knew that she wasn't.

The young officer's thoughts were interrupted as the elder Sister urged them to continue down to the office. Once inside, she closed the door behind them. Sister Beatrice took her seat behind the simple wooden desk, and the Carter and Selby took theirs opposite her.

'What is this about?' the Sister asked.

'It's about Ellie. We believe we have found the men who murdered her parents,' Carter said plainly.

Sister Beatrice was shocked by how casually the words tumbled from his mouth, and for a moment did not know how to respond.

'I see,' she said. 'And you have them in your custody, I trust?'

Carter and Selby exchanged a troubled look, before the sergeant turned and address the nun once more. 'Not quite. They are dead.'

Sister Beatrice sat back in her chair, the shock evident across her face, her mouth dropping open. She crossed herself and rested her hands, fingers locked together, on the table, bowing her head in a quick, silent prayer.

'All of them?' she asked, without looking up.

'That's right,' Carter replied. 'We found their van no more than ten miles from the services where the murders took place. Pulled over on the side of a track that ran away from the main road. Lights were still on, engine was running. But inside, all of them were dead. All of their eyes had been removed.'

The description caused Sister Beatrice to spring from her chair, clasp a hand over her mouth and wave the other towards the officers.

'Please spare me the details, Mr. Carter. You know I do not have a strong stomach.'

'There's more,' PC Selby said as she stood up to offer a hand to the shaken Sister. 'On the front seat of the van, we found this,' she said, reaching into the deep pocket of her coat. From it she took out a small, woollen object. A child's toy. Although she had never seen it, PC Selby – and Sister Beatrice – knew exactly what it was. Since her arrival at Crittenden Hall, much like the night that PC Selby found her, when Ellie had spoken the only thing she had constantly talked about was her ginger-man.

The nun took the knitted toy from Selby's hands and stared at it. Suddenly its woven smile looked malevolent, cruel. Sister Beatrice closer her eyes, repulsed by it, and thrust it back towards PC Selby.

'No, no. You take it. Get it away from me!'

Selby and Carter looked at each other, confused. 'Please excuse me,' Sister Beatrice told them as she hurried to the door. 'Please see yourselves out.' By the time Selby got to the door to look after the troubled old woman, she had gone. There were many doors leading off of the dimly-lit hallway, too many for Selby to guess behind which Sister Abigail now hid behind.

'What was that all about?' Selby asked, still searching the shadows down the hall.

'Got me', Carter shrugged as he stood from his chair. 'Now let's get out of here. There's a hell of a mess to clear up back at the station and it's getting late.'

Carter pushed past Selby and walked briskly down the hall. 'I'll see you back at the car,' he called back to her. Selby paused for a moment longer then made her exit too. As she walked down past the line of bedrooms, she stopped at the only one still with an open door. She peered inside and slowly walked towards the bed. Ellie hadn't moved a muscle since she spied her earlier. She exuded peace, but something else started creeping in Selby's gut as she looked down upon the angelic little girl.

Something nibbled at her from within, a cold gnawing deep inside her. Fear.

Selby gently reached over the sleeping child and tucked the woollen ginger-bread man between Ellie's arms. The toy's face smiled back at her, emptily.

As PC Selby left Crittenden Hall by the large front door and walked back to where the patrol car waited, its engine humming quietly, she stopped and looked back behind her sharply, convinced that she could hear a voice. She strained her ears to listen again, but heard only the wind.

She got back into the car and spent the ride back to the police station in a haze of troubled thought. Something didn't feel right. She closed her eyes and heard the voices again, this time more clearly.

'Run, run as fast as you can. You'll never escape me. I'm the Ginger Man.'

Her eyes snapped open again and she drew in a strangled breath. 'Jesus, Selby!' Carter shouted as he struggled to get control of the steering wheel again. 'What the hell was that? You scared the jeepers out of me!'

'I'm sorry, sir,' Selby replied, 'I don't know what came over me.' Her eyes darted from side to side. She immediately looked out of the window, into the deepening darkness.

Back at Crittenden Hall, Ellie finally slept like a baby. *He* was home, and was never leaving her again.

The End

About the Author: Chris Tetreault-Blay

As a lifelong fan of horror cinema and heavy metal music, it was probably only natural for Chris to discover his love for writing his own stories of the weird and macabre. Having taught himself to play the guitar, his earliest attempts at writing came in the form of song lyrics, which he now posts on his website. However he turned his hand to writing fiction as recently as 2013. After tying together ideas for three short stories, he eventually found himself with his first full novel, *Acolyte*, the first part of The Wildermoor Apocalypse trilogy. He realised his new-found dream of becoming a published author in 2015 and self-published three more titles the following year before signing with Creativia.

Chris moved from Basingstoke to the beautiful Devon countryside, in the south west of England, after graduating from university in 2005. He currently resides in Newton Abbot with his wife and twin children.

Books by Chris Tetreault-Blay:
Acolyte
Blackgang - The Trickerjack Trail
House of Courtenay
The Sowing Season

Links:
Facebook: https://www.facebook.com/ChrisTetreaultBlay/
Twitter: https://twitter.com/ctetreaultblay

Texting at the Gate

By Eve Gaal

"Where am I? And who are all these people?" Al mumbled to no one in particular.

The angels held hands, dancing around what appeared to be a glowing Christmas tree with glittering lights. He looked at their smiles, their elegant wings, robes and halos and thought maybe next time he'd cut back on the hard stuff. Al rubbed his eyes and listened to the upbeat strains of music. "Crappy New Age shit," he muttered to himself, when hearing choral voices accompanied by bells and harps. Minutes later, he heard trumpets but he wasn't sure. Last time he heard trumpets was at a high school football game when Anna Marie kissed him behind the bleachers. The marching band trumpets played out of tune marches that were typically drowned out by the tuba and the bass drum. That was years ago. He patted his breast pocket looking for his cell phone and when he couldn't find it, he angrily spewed curse words into the damp air. High school sucked. Why was he thinking about ancient and bizarre things he had tried to forget?

Anna Marie hadn't meant anything to him—or so he thought. At the time, all he wanted was to get to second base or maybe more but she had a definitive plan. She ended up being the Prom Queen and marrying some rich guy from down South. But Al knew her before she highlighted her hair and wore lipstick. At least he had eked out that memorable make-out session after which he bought her a tube of chap-stick. She laughed at the tiny box with the bow. Disappointment in her eyes when she lifted the lid. She wanted more and deserved more. A castle with a moat, not some dude from her biology class. His

80

life was no fairy tale. There was no Princess, no talking animals and no happily ever after.

The sound of the annoying trumpet blast seemed to cease, replaced by swirls and flourishes of harp music. What the fuck? A man in white clerical looking robes stood next to him clearing his throat and looking upset. "That won't be necessary," the man said in a serious tone.

"What's that? My phone is definitely necessary. What do you know?" Al's head was throbbing and he wondered, how in the hell he ended up at a toga party?

"First of all, I meant cursing is not necessary and secondly, your phone is not necessary either. And as far as your question about 'what do I know?' Hmmm...," the older man had to think about that for a second. "I'd say that's a good one," he said with a small chuckle. "Nonetheless, I'm in charge right now and if you want to enter these gates," he pointed at a fancy entry near the angels, "you might want to sit up and answer some basic questions. But please, could you spare us the profanity?"

"I don't need any help from you," the young man said with an arrogant tone. "Where's my car?"

The old man shrugged. "I have no idea. One of those angels over there probably knows the details of your situation. If you don't cooperate, we have other ways of gaining information but it's so much easier if you can answer the questions yourself."

"What questions?"

"Simple ones for cataloguing purposes such as, your mother and father's name for example."

Though dizzy, Al sat up and looked the bearded, robe-wearing man in the eyes. The man stared back, waiting for him to answer. "How is that any of your business? And what's with the weird music?" His head pounded and he thought he might puke. It felt like the world's worst hangover or the beginning of a brain tumor. "I don't belong in your church and I don't have any idea how I got here. Besides, I don't want to go to your party."

The bearded man smiled. "This is not a church and we happen to like that music. Do you mind standing up?"

Al tried to stand but stumbled back down. "I can't. Leave me alone. Can't you see I don't want whatever it is you're selling?"

The older man tried hiding his grin under his beard. Too many young, belligerent and obstinate fools showed up on Saturday mornings. It was expected and part of a depressing routine. So sad in fact, that he had to find some humor in the situation. "That's too bad because we're not here to sell you anything. You're in a transitional period here and we're just trying to help you so you can continue on with your life."

"Leave me alone," Al yelled. "Is there someone else I can talk to?" He put his head in his hands and wondered where he left his car and cell phone. Doris had wanted to buy some pot and he had one small lid to sell her in his glove compartment. She also wanted to party and he knew what she meant by saying she wanted to party. It meant he'd have a great time. Last time he saw Doris they were so wasted he couldn't even remember if he had a good time or not. She must have had fun or she wouldn't have texted him about coming today. He tried to remember Doris but visions of Anna Marie kept creeping back into his mind. He felt a kinship to Doris. They both had difficulties. They both liked booze.

The guy with the robe walked over to the dancing angels. "Which one of you handled Al Hampton?" They stopped and one of them moved over to the man with the white robe. She whispered something in a hushed tone.

"I see. Can you talk to him? What's that in Psalm 109—something about how cursing seeps into bones like oil? We have to lose the cursing. This one appears to be permeated. Do what you can. He doesn't want to talk to me."

"But I failed," she said sadly. "He was difficult from the time I took over. I always had trouble guarding him and his parents didn't make it any easier."

"So that's why he's here. Explains a lot. We both know it wasn't entirely his fault. Maybe someday he'll take responsibility for his actions but until that time, we know all about how to handle bad boys. In fact, that's one of our specialties," he said with a tinge of pride. "This young man turned to drugs and alcohol because he had a rough time growing up. Am I right?"

The man spoke graciously because it was obvious Al wasn't a boy anymore. Most people his age had grown out of blaming everything on their parents. They either sought counseling or devoted themselves to a worthy cause outside of their inner pain such as rescuing dogs or saving the whales. Some people joined the military or the priesthood and others were married and had large families. "Oh yes, he was beaten repeatedly by his father and his mother always lied to him." The angel was glad there was a glimmer of hope for her lost cause. "His mother is here but she's working off every lie. She's super busy."

The bearded man looked relieved. "That's somewhat positive. The father didn't make it?"

The angel shook her head of curls. "No." She pointed down, making an unhappy face.

Visibly shuddering, his eyes seemed to plead with the seraphim. "Please talk to him? Kid might have a chance. Sounds like a victim of circumstances with some valid excuses. You got him this far and it's only a short way through that gate."

"Ok, I'll do my best," she promised with a beaming smile. Eager to help, she appeared to bow reverently before floating over to Al.

The angel put a delicate hand on Al's shoulder. "Pardon me, may I tell you something?"

"What?" He yelled, pushing her hand away. "Why is everyone whispering around here?"

"Is this better?" she said in a louder tone.

"Much. Are you here to ask me stupid questions too?"

"Well, not exactly. That man with the white robe is Saint Peter. Have you ever heard of him?"

"Get away from me. I don't believe in that horseshit."

"Do you believe in God?"

"No."

She waited a few seconds before continuing. The silence between them seemed endless and she saw impatience growing in his eyes. "See, I know that's not exactly true. You used to say your prayers every night. You loved that fuzzy, stuffed teddy bear that said, "Now I lay me down to sleep, I pray the Lord my soul to keep. Do you remember that?"

Embarrassed, his cheeks turned pink like cheap bubblegum. "That's a load of ass manure. How would you know that? Stop lying." He began looking around and noticed everything looked foggy. The music began to change into chants and his head continued reeling from pain. "I wish you'd go away before I scream," he growled through clenched teeth, putting his arms around his head to block out the repetitive hymns. "Leave me alone."

"Go ahead and scream. We've heard it before—all of it—the yelling—the swear words—the painful tears and sobbing."

"I ain't going to cry, just back off." What he wanted was a beer and his worn outworn-out sofa. Doris wouldn't be bad either.

She waited a few minutes, allowing him to stew in his overblown anger before relaying something important. "Look at me," she said with conviction. He lifted his head and stared into her golden- brown eyes. "Well first of all, I have to tell you about the accident."

"What accident?" Though her voice seemed soothing and her demeanor kind, he felt a commanding presence hover over him the entire time, reminding him of authority. Whether it was the police or his teachers–even his parents—he disliked authority figures. What gave them the right to tell him what to do?

Arms crossed in front of her body, she had the body language and demeanor of a lecturing professor. "Do you remember anything about texting Doris while driving your Dodge Challenger?"

How would she know what kind of car he drove? Was this some sort of court? He looked her in the face and felt shocked about the things she knew. Maybe she was some sort of cop doing undercover work. He vaguely remembered texting Doris and then almost everything went blank. This angel had such a pretty face and enormous eyes. On top of everything, she seemed super smart. Not up to second-guessing her motives, she had his attention. "Are you really an angel?"

She nodded. "Whether you believe in God or not, He forgives you. In fact, He believes in you. That's why you're here. Al, He knows about your dad."

At the word 'dad', his face turned fire engine red and tears squirted from in his eyes. "Sonofabitch." Damn it, he had promised not to cry.

"We know all about it."

Bullshit, bullshit, bullshit she doesn't know anything. There's no way anyone knew about his dad. "No one knows and no one cares," he said aloud. She couldn't know, he thought, wondering if maybe he had slipped up somewhere and what did she mean by 'We?' Did he accidentally tell some loudmouth gossip the entire disgusting, rancid story of his childhood? Nah, this angel had probably hypnotized him. Either that or some chick heard him talking in his sleep and was spreading rumors. He wiped his blurry eyes and tried focusing on the celestial vision in front of him. Maybe this was a nightmare and he'd wake up soon. This person in the white robe had to be some sort of cop—but at least she was nice.

She touched his arm with the palm of her hand in a gentle caress. "We do know and care. Especially God– because that's—that's what He does. I have always worried about you."

"You have?" The more she spoke, the more his attention zoomed onto her luscious lips. There was something familiar about her long, swanlike neck and her tiny ears. Fortunately, his headache began to ebb and the music was now a somewhat pleasing orchestra of harps. As he had never heard harps play, he wasn't entirely sure but it sounded like wind falling over a waterfall. Certain passages reminded him of water trickling over rocks in a creek. The more he listened to the sound of the harp music in the background the more he remembered the few beautiful moments of his short life. Fishing with his mom's dad up in the Sierras or the one time, he went snorkeling off Key West. He inhaled and it felt like a tight belt had fallen away.

"Of course–but we don't call it worry. More like concern. I've always been concerned. Don't you know I'm your guardian angel?"

He took another breath–a deep, deep breath. Suddenly he remembered shattered glass fragments flying through the air. There were sirens blaring and the sound of voices yelling. "Are you saying I died?"

Sighing, she noted comprehension slowly appear on his face and took a step back. "You bumped your head on your windshield." Come on, come on, she prayed softly. You're getting another chance. Take it. "There is life after death. I know you know this and even if you act like you don't care, it's still here for you. It's a better life. It's waiting, right there through that entrance. You're free now." Strumming notes flew into his ear. She pointed at the gate, mumbling something about "happily ever after." All you have to do is answer a few questions."

Saint Peter wandered over and took a look at the man sprawled on the ground. "Any luck, Anna Marie?" Al heard Saint Peter call the beautiful angel Anna Marie and he concentrated on their conversation. It couldn't be the same Anna Marie. That one had married a rich, older gentleman with a giant ranch in Texas and a yacht. But he recognized those lips that he loved so much, her neck that he had strewn kisses all over and ears that he had nibbled. He had vivid memories that had filled many of his dreams with unrequited love and desire. She was a princess with a castle who was supposed to be living happily ever after. He had tuned out the music and even the conversation going around above him as he zoned back in time reliving those kisses.

"Do you mean with the cussing?" asked the angel.

"Among other things," St. Peter answered in a business-like tone. "By the way, his friend Doris is on her way. Maybe she can shed some light on this fellow."

"Doris? " Anna Marie knew almost everything about Doris because there wasn't much to know. Doris dropped out of high school after winning a hard rock karaoke competition. Lately, she worked as a server at a truck stop. She also knew that Al didn't love Doris. "What happened to Doris?"

"She OD'd."

Al looked at his surroundings and surmised that the impressive gateway could very well be the entrance to a castle. Pulling himself up, he stood to face Saint Peter and Anna Marie.

"Al? Are you ready to answer some questions?" Anna Marie whispered.

"Fire away," Al replied, staring into Anna Marie's gorgeous amber eyes. "But wait, I have some questions too, "Do you live in a palace? And are you the same Anna Marie I knew in high school?"

Anna Marie giggled and took hold of his right hand, pulling him towards the gate. "You sure have a lot of questions for a guy with so much to look forward to. Just open your heart and follow me."

The End

About the Author: Eve Gaal

Eve Gaal, M.A. is the author of the romantic novel Penniless Hearts and a faith-based, fantasy novella titled The Fifth Commandment. Her freelance creative writing business is: ***Desert Rocks*** and her inspirational blog: ***Intangible Hearts***. Find links to her stories and poems at http://www.evegaal.com/. Her work has also appeared in ***The Los Angeles Times*** and *Datebook, a weekend edition of The* ***Daily Pilot.*** A precocious child, her dad told her to write about anything and everything, even making sure she had a toy typewriter by age four. Born in Boston, but a longtime Californian, she lives with her husband and two mischievous Chihuahuas.

Books by Eve Gaal:
The Fifth Commandment
Penniless Hearts

Links:
Website: http://www.evegaal.com/

Blossom Shines At Buttercup Bay

By Melanie Mole

Monty shivered as he stepped out of the church and onto the gravel path which led through the churchyard to the small cobbled street. He wrapped his large woolly scarf around him tightly, tucking it under his navy blue duffel coat as he went. Walking briskly, he headed down the steep hill towards home. Past Bob's Plaice, the wonderful fish and chip shop on Fore Street which he had visited last night for a tasty supper of cod and chips washed down with cold lemonade. He remembered how the batter on the fish was crisp and light and the chips dipped in tomato sauce were succulent enough to make his mouth water even now. Bob always seemed to put the right amount of salt and vinegar onto his chips and that was probably why there was often a queue, even in the winter months.

Since his meeting earlier in the day with the choir master about Geraldine, his favourite parishioner's funeral, he'd been feeling sad. He didn't feel like having any chips tonight as a result, and carried on walking.

Along from Bob's Plaice he met Mr. Rose, who owned the village store, leaning against the wall and enjoying a bit of fresh air. "Hello Vicar," he said as he pushed the door open for Monty to enter the store.

"Good evening Mr. Rose," Monty said. "How is Mrs. Rose?"

"Not bad at all thank you Vicar. She'll be even better when I tell her you were wearing that big daft scarf she knitted for you," he said pointing at it with a smile.

"Very warm it is too. Of all the presents I have been given by my parishioners this is the best," Monty said adjusting his scarf slightly around his neck.

"That's the problem, Vicar. All the women round here see a single man like yourself and want to either marry or mother them. I know they mean well but I wish they wouldn't. It can get a bit overpowering for any poor man who becomes the centre of their efforts. But you seem to take it all in your stride, Vicar."

"Oh, I don't mind. If it keeps them happy, then I am happy," he said with a grin.

"Well you let me know if it gets too much Vicar, and then I will have a word with the wife," he smiled handing a shopping basket to Monty with a nod.

"Thank you Mr. Rose," said Monty, and ten minutes later he stood at the counter paying for far too much shopping as he always did. He often regretted buying too much when his arms ached at the weight of it as he got much nearer home. But still he didn't learn and each trip to the store saw him buy just as much as the last.

* * *

Her life was no fairy-tale. There was no princess, no talking animals, no happily ever after. A life-time spinster, Geraldine Howe's life was mundane and boring, and she ploughed on through each day much like the last. Monotony seemed to be her far too frequent friend, especially as it had not been invited to share her days. It had just crept up on her before she had noticed, boring her rigid and testing her patience. Her days consisted of playing the piano for the school choir one afternoon a week and helping with the odd concert, and that was it.

Then along came Blossom, affectionately known as Bloss by most. A gentle donkey who was similar in personality to Geraldine. Their paths crossed unexpectedly when Blossom's previous owner went into hospital and never came out. Doing her neighbour a favour for a few days by looking after her donkey had now turned into one of several years. But she had the barn and the field which had been unused since her father died and so, after some time getting used to the idea, Geraldine decided that Blossom living there was a blessing for them both.

Having been raised with a few sheep and a horse Geraldine was not averse to animals. But, at her time of life, she had neither really expected or wanted to take on another one, especially one which needed to be seen to in all weathers. But Geraldine was good to her word, and when her neighbour had died, there was nobody else to look after her affectionate little donkey. So Geraldine had stepped up and gave it a home. She wasn't really enamoured by its wiry brown coat, but very taken with the way it looked at her, and so a mutual level of affection had soon grown to one where neither really liked to be away from the other for any length of time.

Despite her initial reservations, Geraldine enjoyed spending more time outdoors with Blossom. In the summer, she would sit and read her favourite book to Blossom in the shade of the barn. Although Geraldine knew that she wouldn't understand the words it seemed to give them both comfort. Both gentle and quiet, they spent many hours there just enjoying the company of a likeminded soul. It was an unlikely pairing, but one which worked.

* * *

Monty walked more quickly. He was sure that his arms had grown at least a foot because of the weight of his shopping, but he was determined neither to stop, or drop any of it.

"Why do I always do this?" he asked himself. His arms aching and his breathing not quite as good as it would have been had he only bought the essentials. "When will I learn?."

As he reached the stone steps of the vicarage he wished that he lived on a nice flat road instead of a hill which felt more like a mountain. Where did I put that key? he thought. He sighed knowing that the inevitable search for his key would not only often go on for several minutes, but when he did find it it would be in the first pocket that he had looked in.

Being organized wasn't one of Monty's strengths. He annoyed himself over and over again because on a daily basis he either couldn't find something that should be right in front of him, or would lose them again straight after finding them. This was more of a problem because the vicarage was a large old house where there was plenty of room to lose things. So, the space it provided didn't help him at all, however much he liked living there.

Monty staggered up the wide stone steps and surprised himself by finding his key straight away. He had never quite managed this before and gave a wry smile almost mocking his newfound key finding ability. He unlocked the door, put the tag from his keys between his teeth so that they swung excitedly in front of his mouth, and picked up his heavy bags of shopping before walking inside. Despite the weather the old house wasn't too cold. After all the years that he had lived there he had finally managed to work out the timer for the heating, so all was well.

Monty unceremoniously dropped the shopping onto the old wooden table in the kitchen and closed the heavy red curtains to keep the cold at bay. He breathed a sigh of relief knowing that after putting the shopping away he could relax in front of the television with the other half of the large cottage pie that he had bought yesterday. He loved evenings where he could just relax because with responsibilities such as the evening services and choir practice they were few and far between.

With a nice hot cup of tea and a steaming plate of cottage pie Monty took his place in his battered brown armchair in front of the television. Before switching it on he glanced at the small table by the side of him where the day's post sat. Nothing exciting he thought as he picked up the post and leafed through the envelopes. Then he came to a thicker envelope made of what looked like expensive cream paper which had gold lettering on the back denoting the name of a legal firm. He frowned and hoped that it wasn't bad news.

After finishing his meal Monty put his plate and cutlery into the sink. Returning to his armchair he looked at the letter again and decided to open it.

"Oh my!" he exclaimed. "What on earth do I know about donkeys? And why me?"

With a pained expression creeping across his face he sank further back in his chair as he read the letter again. He sighed and rubbed his forehead with the palm of his hand.

"How on earth can I look after a donkey?" he said. "And why did Geraldine Howe think that I could?" he asked with a bemused look on his face. I know she knew that I liked animals, but this is too much.

Since Geraldine had passed away, just a short while ago, her donkey, Blossom, had been taken care of by well-meaning villagers. Now, it seemed, that Geraldine had set aside money with a request that Monty look after Blossom for the rest of her days, saying that she didn't want either of them to be lonely. The solicitor's letter had set out Geraldine's request as detailed in her will. Monty knew that it was kind in her own way to think of him. But also that having an animal was a great responsibility, especially as he had no idea how to look after a donkey. The letter confirmed that the field and barn where Blossom lived would also be Monty's to do with as he wished after Blossom eventually passed away. It also requested that Monty attend an appointment at the solicitor's office the following Monday morning at 10 o'clock sharp.

For the following few days Monty didn't sleep well. His unexpected bequest had played on his mind and he knew that from today he must step up to the plate and take on his new responsibilities for Blossom. He had driven into the nearest town to find a book shop that might have a book on how to care for a donkey. But his journey was without success,so, he had looked on the internet and eventually found just what he was looking for, and had ordered it to arrive the next day.

That had been two days ago now, and since then Monty had devoured it from cover to cover. Determined to both learn how to care for Blossom to the best of his ability, and not to let Geraldine down, he had learned about Hoof Deformity, Laminitis, and Grass Sickness otherwise known as Equine Dysautonomia, and it all seemed a little scary to him.

But in those few days since he had received the solicitor's letter he had come to terms somewhat with what he would need to do to keep Blossom well and happy. He was determined to face any challenges head on for both her sake and his. He had decided that he would make a determined effort to get the best information and help, including that of Mr. Darby, the village vet. He hoped and prayed that he could do it.

* * *

Monty walked nervously into the office of Nevis and Brown. He hadn't been into a solicitor's office for a long time and so was a little nervous.

"Good morning sir," the receptionist said with a smile. "Please take a seat and Mr. Nevis will see you soon."

"Thank you" Monty said smiling awkwardly.

He leafed nonchalantly through a magazine from the table in front of him. Not really reading it, more perusing it than anything.

"Mr. Nevis will see you now sir," motioning towards the door to her left.

Monty nodded and made his way through the door.

During the next half an hour Mr. Nevis explained what Geraldine had requested including the money he had been left to look after Blossom, and that the field and barn where she lived would be Monty's to do with as he wished when Blossom had finally passed. Monty nodded but didn't really take in much of the information. He still couldn't quite believe that he would be Blossom's owner and all of the responsibilities that that entailed.

On his way home, despite being in best clothes, Monty decided to visit Blossom. She knew him quite well as he had visited with Geraldine several times. So when he leaned over the gate to her field and called her name, she plodded over to him without a fuss.

"Well who would have thought it old girl?" he asked as he patted Blossom's back. "It's just you and me now."

Blossom brayed loudly and shook her head, looking up at him with her big brown eyes and beautiful long eye lashes. Monty smiled, "Don't worry old girl. It will all be OK."

* * *

The weeks came and went, and life moved on. Monty was feeling much more confident in his abilities to care for Blossom, and except for the time that he spent at her field, his life ran on as normal. That was until he received a call from the Emma Smythe, the headmistress of the village school.

"Good morning Vicar, and how are you this fine day?" asked Emma.

"Very well thank you," said Monty. "You?"

"As well as can be expected with a school full of excitable children."

"I'm sure they are, with the Christmas holidays soon approaching."

"Quite," Emma answered. "That is actually the reason that I am calling, Vicar. I was just checking that Blossom will be able to perform her usual duties this year at the Christmas concert?"

"What duties?" Monty asked.

"Where she carries Mary as she makes her way into the stables for the nativity scene."

"Oh. I hadn't thought of that," Monty glanced at his reflection in the mirror over the fireplace. "I…I mean I know that she always does play a part, but had forgotten about it entirely, this being the first year that I am in charge of her so to speak." He sighed inwardly to himself at the thought of it, but at the same time knowing that they couldn't let the children down.

"The dress rehearsal is Tuesday afternoon Vicar. I take it that you can both attend?."

Monty quickly checked his diary. "Yes of course," he replied.

"About 2pm then Vicar. Come to the side entrance and we will let you both in when the children are settled in their places."

"Yes. OK. See you then."

* * *

The next few days came and went, and Monty busied himself with his usual duties. The only difference was that he had given Blossom a good wash and brushed her coat. She seemed to quite enjoy it he thought. They were gradually forging a trusting relationship which he was pleased about. Monty wasn't too worried about walking her the short distance along the lane from her field to the school. He was thankful that Blossom was quite a docile creature who seemed to enjoy any attention given to her from those passing by. They walked slowly along the lane but were at the school in just a few minutes.

Judging from Emma's smile, she was pleased that they had arrived.

"Just in time Vicar," Emma said with a smile as they reached the verge by the side entrance. She opened the large oak doors and lead the way into the main hall of the school where the dress rehearsal was to take place. A long, gently rising slope at the back of the stage was where Blossom would make her grand entrance. Monty was pleased that it was one which she could easily walk on, not wanting her to slip before she got onto the stage. Blossom didn't disappoint, walking up it like an old pro. When she got to the top and onto the side of the stage the children all welcomed her warmly. Blossom seemed to lap up the attention and Monty smiled to see her so content. It was nice to see her so settled he thought.

Monty looked at Emma as she clapped her hands.

"Come along now children, all settle down. We have a lot to get through this afternoon." They watched as the children all scurried into their allocated places and sat to await further instructions.

Monty had already been informed that John, one of the older children, would lead Blossom the few paces from stage right to where she would stand for the rest of the show. Monty was pleased because his only job was to sit in the wings at the side of the stage and make sure that nothing unforeseen happened along the way. He nodded his approval when given his instructions and settled on the chair as directed. His smile grew as he listened to each performer say their lines. Some making mistakes, but not seeming to mind too much.

Throughout the rehearsal Monty saw that Emma encouraged the children beautifully, knowing that for some it was a quite daunting task. He thought how pleased she looked at how even the little ones had coped, and he smiled when she told them that they could all choose a book to take home for the night in recognition of their sterling efforts. They all filed back to their classrooms looking pleased with themselves. Monty waved as they went and patted Blossom's side.

"Thank you so much Vicar," Emma said.

"You're most welcome Emma," Monty said with a smile.

"Blossom was her usual calm self. We really are lucky that you agreed to let her attend."

"Think nothing of it Emma. See you on the big day."

"Yes Monty. See you on Friday," Emma said, nodding and leading them back out of the large oak doors at the side of the building.

Monty and Blossom walked back to her field peacefully. Even when a large lorry had come a bit too close to them she had just carried on walking as though she didn't have a care in the world. She was placid and calm throughout and Monty loved that about her.

* * *

The day of the performance quickly arrived and Monty made sure that Blossom looked her best again. They had received their instructions to be at the side entrance of the school at exactly 9.50am. Knowing that it would only take them a few minutes to walk there Monty led Blossom from her field in time to have a gentle meander along the way. She enjoyed the new smells and all was well. Monty could see the sea lapping below them in the bay. Even though it was nearly Christmas the sun shone on it making it shimmer. He thought that it looked beautiful.

He saw that Emma looked flustered as she welcomed them.

"Sorry for the wait," she said as she opened the door. "I was trying to get the shepherds into line."

"Oh, don't worry about that," Monty said with a smile. 'We are here and ready for Blossom's performance as planned'.

Emma smiled and ushered them towards the slope at the back of the stage.

"Come on old girl. It's time for you to play your part." Then he gently led Blossom up the slope towards the stage.

Within a few minutes the crowd had taken their seats and an excited air had filled the room. Monty stroked Blossom's side and he felt her relax. Then he handed the reins to John for him to walk Blossom the few steps onto the stage.

Emma appeared a little flustered, but clapped her hands together briskly and smiled at the crowd. There were many familiar faces, and also a few that he hadn't seen before. As Emma looked around the room the whispers lessened and everyone looked towards the children up on the stage with anticipation.

"Welcome everyone," Emma said enthusiastically. "I am sure that you are all going to enjoy this year's performance. The children have worked incredibly hard and I am sure that you will give them a warm welcome," and she smiled and motioning towards the stage as the crowd clapped loudly.

Monty listened to Emma as she explained, "As usual we haven't charged for tickets for the show. However, we shall be collecting donations afterwards by the exit doors at the back of the hall. As usual all proceeds go towards school outings for the children," she said pointing towards them. "Now, if you are all ready, we shall begin. The first carol is The Holly and The Ivy."

Emma turned to look at the children and signaled for them to stand up. She then nodded towards Mrs. Dent who was sat waiting at the piano and the music began.

Monty joined in the singing heartily. He had always liked the Christmas carols and so he was as enthusiastic as usual, smiling broadly as he sang and looking around him admiring the wonderful costumes and set. This is a good day he thought.

Blossom had behaved impeccably and all was well. The children were all doing as they were meant to, and everyone in the audience seemed duly impressed. Emma smiled at them all and gave them an encouraging smile.

It was soon time for Blossom to carry Mary over to the manger. Monty watched as she went, secretly proud of how she had done exactly as asked. Mary sat by the manger and Joseph was just about to speak. The shepherds were also about to enter from the back and walk towards the manger to deliver their presents to baby Jesus.

Suddenly there was a deafening bang. One of the shepherds had tripped and fallen into quite a large piece of scenery and before anyone could help him the scenery had come crashing down towards the floor with yet another loud bang sending puffs of dust up into the air that made everyone who was near enough cough and splutter. Luckily the falling piece of scenery had missed both the children and animals. But in fright many of them had started to scream loudly and to run towards the front of the stage.

Parents dashed to help them down onto the floor below the stage, comforting them and telling them that that they would be fine. But as they did, Blossom bolted from her charge and made a run for it. Monty, who after too many cups of tea, had been to the lavatory when the commotion started, came back to the stage just in time to see John flying along the floor whilst trying with all his might to hold onto Blossom. '

"Oh no! Oh dear. What on earth is going on?' Monty asked with a bemused look on his face as he saw the mayhem and flung himself as fast as could towards Blossom. Unfortunately, Monty wasn't quick enough and so Blossom carried on running to the front of the stage and down the steps towards the audience. John had managed to keep hold of Blossom's rein until she jumped off of the stage and then he had lost hold of it. Luckily, he had landed in the lap of Mrs. Shields the nursery class teacher, so although he was a little shaken, he was actually unhurt except for a slightly grazed leg.

Amidst all of the confusion Monty managed to finally grab hold of Blossom's bridle and to calm her down. It was probably only seconds, but had seemed like hours. He tried to move her to the back of the hall as quickly as possible whilst dodging screaming children and bemused looking parents. Despite the chaos Monty managed to get Emma's attention. He signaled that he was going to take Blossom home and Emma nodded.

In the meantime, John had thought it highly amusing to have been flying through the air like an aeroplane all helped along by Blossom. He thought it even more funny when he had landed in his teacher's lap, especially as she hadn't seemed at all amused by it. In fact, her horrified expression made him giggle. The more Mrs. Shields grimaced, the more John laughed.

As his horrified mother approached him she saw that he was laughing almost to the point of not being able to control himself. He rocked back and forth and was pointing at Mrs. Shields enthusiastically as he guffawed. Then one by one the other children started to laugh and point at her too. The shepherds were particularly enthusiastic in their efforts which made Mrs. Shields blush. She had always hated being the centre of attention and by this time she was visibly squirming.

"Stop that," John's mother said as she grabbed him and removed him from Mrs. Shield's lap. "You are embarrassing us."

But at the look of John laughing, despite the humiliation for everyone involved, she couldn't help but eventually smile. Probably in part due to the relief that he was OK after his unexpected flight, but also because the laughter in the hall was now almost at fever pitch. Even Mrs. Shields was laughing, although she didn't really know why.

Monty saw that Emma was still both in a state of shock, and looking completely horrified. She couldn't believe how everyone was behaving. She'd had great expectations about the concert and now it was ruined. To say that she was deeply embarrassed was an understatement. Emma appeared frustrated. The more she tried to quieten everyone the more they laughed. She could see that even Mrs. Shields, who was normally such a staid type of person, was laughing so much that she had tears streaming down her face.

"Come along now everyone," Emma said. "We can't sit here all day. Let's start making our way out of the hall," ushering them gently towards the door. Emma didn't expect anyone to leave donations, but the children duly rattled their donation buckets anyway. She tried to signal to them to stop. But her efforts fell on deaf ears.

* * *

"Now look here old girl," Monty said looking at Blossom as they arrived back at her field. "That was a fiasco of epic proportions. You have no idea what an awful lot of trouble we will be in, and I will be the one who will have to explain it," he said rubbing his hand against his chin. "Oh well. Nothing can be done about it right this minute so I guess it's time to put you back in the barn for the night." He led Blossom into her barn and closed the gate. "Goodnight old girl. Sleep tight."

Monty awoke late the next morning and was pleased when he realised that although it was Saturday, there were no weddings to attend to. He smiled to himself, turned over, and pulled his quilt up over his shoulders to keep warm. Then the smile was wiped off of his face when he remembered what had happened at the concert the day before.

"Oh gosh." he said. "I've got a lot of making up to do today. But first I need a hearty cooked English breakfast to help me. If you are going to be enemy number one then you might as well be it on a nice full stomach."

Within ten minutes he had showered, shaved, dressed and was walking into the kitchen whistling to himself. He drew back the heavy old curtains and opened his fridge. His face dropped as inside it was only a pint of milk, a half-eaten banana, and some butter. I won't get far on that he thought.

"Time to visit the Harbour Grill for my breakfast then," he said as he put on his coat, and walked down the steps at the front of his house and headed down the hill towards the harbour.

Despite choosing to have his breakfast at the Harbour Grill, more out of necessity than anything, Monty still wanted to lie low for the day. He chose a table by the window and sat facing the harbour so that he hopefully wouldn't have to speak to anyone else who was there.

However, in a small seaside town like Buttercup Bay word soon got around. He knew that meant he would probably be the talk of the town right now, and that was something which he neither relished or wanted.

"Newspaper Vicar?" Molly the waitress asked handing it to him with a grin. "I see your Blossom was the star of yesterday's show."

Monty smiled awkwardly. Not wanting to agree, or to get into that conversation. He took the newspaper and turned back to face the harbour.

'No!' he exclaimed. 'This can't be happening,' Monty said looking at the front page of the local newspaper. In large letters it said, Donkey Steals the Show. "Mortified. I'm absolutely mortified."

Monty hoped that nobody heard him. He didn't want to engage in conversation with anyone about it, and certainly didn't want to answer their questions, or to explain what happened. Because in reality it all happened far too quickly for him to really know much about it. Plus, the fact that he wasn't actually by the stage at the time as he should have been only made it worse.

Monty felt a tap on his shoulder. He turned around slowly to see Emma staring at him.

"Emma!" exclaimed Monty. "I…I'm so sorry for what happened yesterday. Mortified in fact."

Monty shrunk a little in his chair as he looked at her, wanting the ground to open up and swallow him so that he didn't have to face the consequences quite yet. He wasn't ready. He needed to digest what happened himself first.

Emma sat down next to him and looked him straight in the eye with a fixed stare. Her eyes met his and he took a sharp intake of breath.

"What happened yesterday?" she asked.

"I...I...Well, I don't really know," Monty said. "One minute everything was fine, and the next minute there was complete chaos."

"That's not how I see it Monty," said Emma. "That's not how I see it at all."

Monty felt his chest tighten slightly and he wanted to bolt for the door. He didn't like confrontation of any kind, and if Emma wanted to be funny about what happened then maybe she shouldn't have insisted that he had so many cups of tea when they had arrived. Because if she hadn't, then perhaps he wouldn't have needed to go off to the toilet mid performance, and he might have been able to control Blossom instead of her running off of the stage.

"I have just one thing to say to you Monty," Emma said.

Monty felt his stomach flip and he fidgeted in his chair. Emma sounded angry and as he hadn't expected to see her today he wasn't prepared to be berated in public.

"Yesterday was amazing Monty," she said smiling. "The best Christmas concert ever actually."

Monty was stunned. "What...What do you mean Emma?"

"Well, as you probably guessed, I wasn't expecting anyone to be either happy about the events of yesterday, or to leave any donations. But to my surprise, and despite the fact that the concert was only half way through when it unceremoniously finished, parents have been giving me positive comments last night and this morning."

"Really? I can't believe it."

"Yes, really Monty. But even better than that, the donations that everyone left after the concert yesterday were almost double what we had hoped for. Based on the previous few years, we hadn't expected anywhere near that amount."

"That's amazing Emma," gushed Monty. "I thought that you would be furious."

"Well, initially I wasn't that impressed with how things turned out. But when I realised that everyone seemed to enjoy it I decided to take it all in my stride. To accept it so to speak."

"Good for you," said Monty. "I'm sorry if we embarrassed you yesterday."

"You didn't. In fact you could say that Blossom stole the show...and I couldn't be happier!"

The End

About the Author: Melanie Mole

Melanie dreams of a place where we are all doing what makes our soul come alive. Where getting up each day is a pleasure rather than a chore, and where life is calmer for us all. These two books are only the start of a series exploring how writers can help themselves in an all too busy world.

This year Melanie has started to branch out into writing fiction. Her story in this anthology is part of her *Buttercup Bay* series about a quaint coastal village in England.

Red Belly

By Natalie J Case

When the night skies light with waves of color and cast the world in shadows of deep purple and blue, a hush settles over the land. Days and nights become one for as many as ten turns. No one travels, business stops. It is the time of the Fall, a name reminiscent of our long-ago history when the people believed that the sky itself was falling to the ground.

The people here are superstitious, even now so far removed from that place of ignorance. They hold to their stories of the Fall, how it began as a sign of a god's wrath, and how hundreds caught outside as it began fell ill and died. Few brave the world outside when the lights shower down. It is said that ill fortune comes to those who exchange money during the time of the Fall.

Even more so to those who would cross the threshold between death and life. A child born during the fall is feared, so much so that mothers will give birth in secret and declare the child was born just before or just after.

My mother, while a poor woman born of a poor woman, cared nothing for superstitions. She was strong, both physically and in her mind. She lived in a cottage on the grounds of the palace with her own mother, who was employed shepherding the children of those who lived and worked there.

It was a rumor that Mother was the product of an illicit union, an affair between my grandmother and a noble boy. A rumor given credence by the color of Mother's skin. In a world where skin color divided class lines, with those of pale complexion at the bottom, and the vibrant hues at the top, the green and blue that painted mother's skin, even though pale in comparison, told the world that she was of unusual parentage.

Mother was raised there, among the palace children, given space among them by virtue of her skin, and allowed to learn with them, play with them. She had designs on entering government when she was in her teens, an opportunity she would not have had were she as white as her mother.

That changed abruptly for her when she was nearly of age to begin. There was an opening offered to her once she passed the age of majority, in the office of a Counselor from the lower provinces. However, before her day came, she discovered herself to be with child. That in and of itself would not have kept her from the position, but like her mother before her, Mother's chosen lover was from a class above her station. The man was married, his wife barren. When it was discovered that Mother would give him the child that she could not, the wife demanded that she be sent away from the palace.

Thus it was, that I was born.

On the fifth night of the Fall, on an island with little more than the hut she lived in and no one to aid her, she gave birth to me. It was a sign, she said.

She named me Aruk-na, which in the old tongue means Red Belly. From my first memory, she told me that destiny had touched me and one day, I would ascend beyond my humble birth.

I do not believe that this is what she expected for me, as I watch the end of the Fall from the window of my tower prison, many years and many miles from that beginning.

Mine is not one of those stories that are told to children, with princesses and dragons and true love to win the day, no matter the odds, though there were all three of these things in the course of the journey from that small island to this prison.

It begins there, on that island where I lived with my mother from the day I was born until the day that she died. I was seventeen when it happened. She had been to town only the week before, a journey that required a boat to shore, and a walk to the nearest transport, which then took her into the town of Jasmire, where whispers followed her until she left again.

The illness came with her, and in the small hours of the day, before the sun had stirred to streak the black skies with gold, she rattled her last breath and died.

I was alone with only the stories my mother told me to guide my next steps. I took her body to shore and buried her in a stand of trees not far from the road. There was no need to mark her grave, I had no intention of returning.

My steps took me into town, a place I had visited from time to time, but never found any affection for. The only modernity it boasted was the transport line that took people into the capital and back again.

I boarded that transport with the money Mother left behind and all my worldly possessions contained in the small bag I slung over my shoulder. I didn't know what to expect. I had never been beyond Jasmire.

The ride was quiet. No one knew that I was a daughter of the palace or the nature of who I was. My skin spoke softly that I was from a class well above most of the people in Jasmire. The pale green that covered my body was enhanced with bright emerald along my hairline and patches of sapphire on my neck and hands. I imagine had they known that my stomach was covered in crimson, they would find reason to talk. These were the colors of my parentage and the green and blue afforded me a privacy among the less brightly colored citizens around me. The red, however, was a different story. It too spoke of my parentage. It marked Mother's telling of my origins as true.

The quiet suited me fine. I was never one for polite conversation for the sake of conversation. When we stopped in the city, I stood and made for the doors, and the others stood back, letting me pass first.

The sights and smells were different than I had known. Near the station there was the smell of closeness, people and waste, burning trash and food cooking. I wrinkled my nose in distaste and moved away quickly. The streets were narrow with buildings too tall and too close, making the world seem dark and dangerous.

I knew nothing about the city aside from stories my mother told, but I had come wanting to see the palace, to see the place my mother had come from. I knew that the palace lay at the center of the city, a sprawling complex of buildings that housed the seats of government and home to those descended from the old lines of nobility and royalty.

They were revered by the populace, even centuries after the monarchy gave way to the complex system of Counsels and Senate that ruled today.

I made my way deeper into the city, and the close, crowded streets gave way to broad avenues and single family homes, laying low behind the walls of apartment buildings and tenements that housed the less fortunate and under pigmented. Neighborhoods punctuated with parks that grew deep carpets of scarlet grass adorned with burst of yellow and orange flowers and canals of crystal clear water spread inward, each becoming more opulent than the next.

At long last I came to the river Mar that ran through the city and down to the coast. In the distant past, it had been diverted to circle around the palace, creating an island upon which the world could focus its gaze. There were seven bridges that crossed the twenty feet of water, making the palace appear to be the center of a wheel.

Each bridge served a purpose. Two of them were open to the public, allowing those who needed to visit government offices for work or other purposes to come and go. Two were restricted for only those who lived in the palace. The western gate was open only to those who supplied the palace with material goods and the last two were maintained strictly for military use.

It was late in the day as I reached the side of the river, content for the moment to merely sit beside the water and look at the palace. It was as my mother described, shining and opulent, it's walls washed in gold. It was dazzling as the suns moved toward the distant mountains.

I would need to find shelter for the night. Reluctantly, I turned from the pull of the palace and inquired of someone out walking with their brightly colored children as to a place I could rent a room. I was directed to an inn where I secured a room for the next several nights. It left me with only a little money.

As night descended, I realized I would need a job, but with no experience and no family name, it would be difficult. I had another option, of course.

I could present myself at the palace, bare my crimson stomach and demand I be accepted as a member of the royal family. Done publicly, they would have no choice. Heat rose in my cheeks as I considered the spectacle. There would be scandal, that a royal child had been born outside the palace would see to it. The woman who sent my mother away would be vilified, my place as a royal daughter undeniable.

I suppose there are many who would do so. I found myself wondering what life that would give me. What did the royal family do, after all? Sure, some of them ran charities and the like, but the others?

No, I was not made for a passive life. I would find my own way... and once I was settled I would seek out an audience with the Prince Regent. I slipped into bed that night with a calm determination.

As luck would have it, I would find the next chapter of my life on the streets of the capital on the day that I was left without a roof to cover me. I had spent the last of my money on food, a crusty loaf of bread and a warm cup of soup, and had once again packed up all of my meager belongings, walking down to the river to gaze upon the palace as I did every day as the suns inched closer to the horizon.

I sat on a bench and ate the last of my bread and contemplated what I would do next. I was deep in thought when I felt the eyes of someone on my face. I looked up thinking for a moment that I had lost my ability to process thought. The deepest purple eyes I had ever seen looked into me and deep indigo lips smiled ever so slightly, making the world stand still.

It took me a moment to realize she was speaking to me. I blinked rapidly and tore my gaze from her face, taking in the rest of her now. Her neck and the part of her chest I could see was brightly emerald and her hair was nearly the color of the night. I cleared my throat. "I'm sorry," I said. "I didn't hear you."

She smiled in earnest then, and my heart nearly choked me. "I said, tonight is the first night of the Fall. You should get inside."

I looked up at the sky, searching for the first hints that the spectacular show of lights would be starting. "I am unafraid of the lights." I said softly, looking down at the backs of my hands which seemed such a pale blue beside her indigo that I wanted to hide them. "Besides, I have no inside to go to."

Color rose in her face. "That will not do." She held out a hand that was a softer blue with red freckles. So, she was a royal daughter as well. "Come with me. I will shelter you until the Fall has ended."

"I could not ask such a thing." I demurred.

"You did not ask," she responded, taking my hand from my lap and tugging me to my feet. She pulled my hand through her crooked arm and began walking. I had little choice but to walk with her. As we approached the bridge, she turned her face and with her lips nearly on my ear, she said, "My name is Kenwith."

I couldn't give her my real name. I swallowed the name and offered my mother's instead. "I am called Chenna."

"Come along, Chenna, and we will become fast friends."

She was nearly five years my senior, I would learn. The second daughter of a second daughter of a second son. So distant from the actual crown as to be considered merely noble, not royal, no matter the color of her freckles. Her rooms in the palace were big enough to hold four of the house I grew up in.

She had a servant make up a guest room in her suite, and we sat before a fire as the night fell and the Fall began, speaking of her day spent helping her mother's pet project in a tenement building near the edge of the city, and I did my best not to display my ignorance.

"But you haven't a clue about any of it, have you?" she asked after a while. "And on I prattle. Tell me of you, then. How is it you come to be without a home to shelter you during the Fall?"

"Oh, I have a home." I said, a bit defensively. "But it is far from here, and I have no interest in returning to it."

"Far from here? Outside the city?" Her eyes widened and she grabbed my hand. "I have never been outside the city. Mother forbids it, says there is danger enough in the slums."

"Your mother is wise. You would not like the country." I said, hoping we could move on. The heat of her skin on mine was palpable and I swallowed before reluctantly tugging back my hand. "As I said, the Fall does not scare me. I have been outside in it before."

Her eyes sparkled with mischief. "Oh, there is no danger in the Fall itself, only in the value of your reputation should you be found outside in it."

I was smitten from the first, as Kenwith was intelligent as well as beautiful and in the nine days of the Fall we spent many hours together. She showed me into the palace library on the fourth day, and the vast expanse of knowledge it contained swept me away.

It was that library that would seal my fate and lead me to this tower prison that has become my home. I lost hours there, reading ever older chronicles of our land, our people. Even when the Fall had ended and it was safe for me to leave again, I stayed.

Slowly, Kenwith introduced me to the collected remains of our royalty and nobility. Some of the names were familiar from my mother's stories, others were new and unknown. They accepted me, based on the colors of my skin, sorting me into the various families based on the dominance and location of those colors.

I had been there nearly two months when the day came that I met the man I assumed to be my father. Kenwith and I were in one of the many gardens, sitting beside a waterfall fed by the river, tumbling into a pool that in turn fed a stream that flowed back out into the river.

I was reading from some ancient tome I had borrowed from the library, my head filled with tales of dragons and flying cats when a shadow fell over me.

I looked up, surprised by the height of the man. I stood, letting my gaze shift upward.

He wore a jacket of dark navy blue that opened to show of the crimson oval on his stomach, and had slits in the arms to show flashes of the indigo beneath. His eyes sparkled a deep violet, lashed in lush black. His face was a dusty pale blue, but for a slash of green that accentuated his jawline. His hair had once been black, like Kenwith's, but was now a mix of dark gray and white. He wore it long and plaited in a style I had seen on others.

Kenwith stood quickly, inclining her head in respect. "Uncle, I was not expecting you."

He turned his intense gaze from me to Kenwith. "I heard rumors that you had brought someone new to us, without establishing her parentage." He seemed amused more than angry. His fingers caught on my chin, turning my face so that he could see my colors. "Who are you then?"

I licked my lips. If this was indeed my father, he would know my mother's name, yet I still felt compelled to hide my given name. "I am Chenna." I said, lifting my eyes to meet his. "And my parentage is something of a mystery."

His eyebrow lifted and his gaze swept over me. "Chenna?"

I stepped back a half pace, pulling my face from his hand. "It was my mother's name. I trust you knew her. She grew up here, in the palace."

His gaze tightened and his hand was swift, grabbing at my shirt and tugging it up to reveal the red skin of my stomach. He cursed in the old language, making Kenwith's face darken and flush.

My heart raced and I nearly fled the garden, but he was holding to my shirt. For a long moment, he stood and stared before his eyes snapped up to mine. He dropped my shirt. I couldn't read his face.

He turned away from me without another word and left the garden. Kenwith looked at me with wide eyes and I wanted to turn away. I hadn't lied to her, only kept a secret, and yet I felt as if I had betrayed her somehow.

She took my hand, drawing me further into the garden, turning me away from the path where he had appeared and disappeared. Her hand caressed softly over my face and concern seemed to take up residence in her eyes. "You are the child of the women that his first wife sent away." It wasn't a question. "Why did you not announce yourself?"

I looked down at the grass and shook my head lightly. "I have no need to make trouble, for myself or…"

"He has no heir, Chenna. He will not turn you away." She lifted my face. "You are family, and royal."

"The only family I have known is dead. I am only the unwanted daughter of an unsanctioned dalliance with a low-born woman who worked in a low-level government office." I pulled away from her and went back to retrieve the book I had been reading. I was half certain I would be sent away.

"Where are you going?" Kenwith asked as I walked toward the door that led to the long corridor that would take me to the library.

"To return this book." I replied.

She followed me, running to catch up and capturing my hand. "I won't let you run away," she said breathlessly. "Stay. You don't have to announce yourself. Just don't go."

We stopped, just outside the mammoth doors to the library. "Why?" I asked.

She moved in closer, her eyes sparkling. "I should think my reasons are obvious," she said softy. Her lips brushed mine and the racing thoughts in my head stopped cold, leaving me dizzy.

"Ken." I breathed the name, my eyes fluttering open before I'd realized they had closed.

"Stay," she whispered.

I found myself nodding in agreement and when she moved away, she brought me with her, hand in hand as we left the library to its silence and returned to her suite.

I kept to myself in the days that followed, staying in her suite, but I was not to be allowed my solitude. We were summoned to dinner on the occasion of Dukka-no, an ancient holiday commemorating the first dragon, born of blood and fire and given by the ancient gods to secure our lands from advancing enemies.

Mother had told me the stories, the same as she had all the others about the royal family, about the gods and the various religions that had grown and wilted in our lands. I had never taken part in traditional celebrations however.

Kenwith and I bathed and I allowed her to dress me, though I balked at the gown when I first saw it. The dress was stunning, but that wasn't my hesitation. Like my father's clothing that day in the garden, the sweeping cloth that would cover my breasts parted to allow the red of my belly to be seen.

It took her cajoling to get me into the gown, it's white cloth and gold embroidery making my skin seem a deeper green, and showing off the red skin of my belly in a most regal way. Kenwith called her servant in to fix my hair while she dressed in something much less dramatic. I felt out of place beside her, a fraud of some kind.

Heads turned as we walked through the palace and out into courtyard. People whispered as we entered the residential wing of the royal family. Kenwith's hand slipped into mine, her palm damp with sweat, making me realize that she too was nervous.

We were met in a spacious lobby adorned with golden dragons and statues of the last kings and queens and escorted to a dining room where my father and others were already seated.

"The Lady Kenwith and her companion, the Lady Chenna."

I cleared my throat. "Aruk-na." I said, my voice sounding harsh in the cold air of the room. "Aruk-na is the name my mother gave me. Chenna is the name I chose."

The man who was my father stood, welcoming us to the table. "Aruk-na is a fitting name. Your mother never was one to hide behind social conventions."

I inclined my head as I took my place with Kenwith beside me. The woman beside my father stood, dressed in the red robes of a priestess of the old faith. She lifted her hands in supplication and pronounced a blessing in the old tongue, speaking of the coming of dragons and the fires of faith.

When she finished, servants approached with plates of food and we began to eat. It was quiet for a long time before a woman a little older than Kenwith leaned toward me from across the table. "Tell us, Lady Chenna, where have you been hiding yourself?"

"Lady Kenwith was kind enough to offer me the shelter of her rooms when she found me on the first night of the Fall." I responded, reaching for my glass of water.

"And before that?" The man who spoke sat two seats down from me. I recognized his face from portraits I had seen around the palace, "Tyndor," Kenwith whispered to me. He was a descendant of dukes and earls.

"Before that I lived far away from here, on an island with my mother. Once she died, I chose to come visit the city that she loved. And hated."

"She had reason to hate us," my father said. "As do you."

Kenwith took my hand under the table, squeezing it lightly. "I have no hate in my heart." I responded. I glanced aside at Kenwith and lifted our joined hands to kiss her knuckles. "Indeed, since coming here, I have discovered love."

A murmur rippled around the table, whether of acceptance or discomfort, I couldn't be sure. My father caught my eye, a slight smile on his lips. I had no idea what it meant.

The talk turned to courtly gossip and governmental things and over the course of the meal, Kenwith whispered names and positions to me. My father, Larun-do was the last remaining Prince, the patriarch of the royal family. The priestess was Hella-ma, a royal cousin who was sent to the church when she was younger than I. The woman who had first spoken was called Casta, a cousin of the Prince.

My father's third wife sat beside him. She was young, her skin a darker green than mine with bright blues that accented her eyes and lips. Kenwith told me her name was Dyra, and a controversial choice for the Prince as she was more closely related than many were comfortable with.

Rounding out the rest of the table was a man barely older than I, his skin a soft blue but for the yellow across his forehead, who Kenwith said was nearly as distant a relation as she, but had gained status though his work in the Senate. Billow was his name. And lastly was a boy of perhaps thirteen, who was a nephew to the prince, the presumed heir, since my father had yet to produce a child of his own lineage.

I clung to Kenwith's hand, uncomfortable and unable to decide how best to extricate myself from the situation. At long last, the dishes were cleared and Larun-do stood, thanking everyone for joining him. The priestess gave another blessing, short and simple, and one by one the gathered people began to disperse.

"Chenna, a moment."

I glanced up as Kenwith and I stepped back from the table. My father beckoned me with two fingers. I kissed Kenwith's knuckles and went to him, allowing myself to be drawn to a side room with him and the priestess.

He drew the door closed and smiled at me. "I wanted to apologize for the other day, when we met. I was taken off guard. You look much like your mother."

I wasn't sure how to respond, but I nodded in acceptance of his apology.

"I don't know how much you have followed the politics of late, but you return to us at a trying time."

"I haven't much head for politics." I confessed. "And being raised as I was, know only the stories of our past, not the complexity of today's governance."

He nodded, looking to Hella-ma. She turned to me. "We are at a place of convergence, Chenna. There is much corruption within the houses of congress, and the people are clamoring for it to be cleansed. There are many returning to the old faith, and there is talk of dragons returning."

"They are all dead, are they not?" I asked, confused.

"Many believe it so."

I watched them, trying to discern what they were not saying. After a long silence, my father turned to me. "There are dragons, Aruk-na. Hiding in plain sight. But we become fewer with each generation."

I narrowed my eyes at him, discerning his meaning on an instinctual level.

"Tell me," Hella-ma said, "were you born during the Fall?"

I nodded. "I was, on the fifth night of the Fall."

"It is true then." Hella-ma walked away, to a pedestal upon which a large book rested. "She is the sign that the time has come."

"I'm not sure I understand." I said, stepping toward the book and the priestess.

"When the last dragon queen stepped down, handing over the governing of her people to the people, she warned that if the people should fall to corruption, she would send them a new dragon, born of the Fall, with a belly as red as her own, untouched by the corruption."

I shook my head. "I am no dragon." I countered. "I am a woman, as was my mother."

Larun-do took my hand. "Your belly says otherwise. It is the mark of the blood that fills you."

I pulled my hand free. "I don't believe you."

"I understand you frequent our library." Hella-ma said, stopping me as I made for the door. "If we are right, there is proof to be found there."

"What proof?" I asked, despite myself.

"Meet me there tomorrow morning and I will show you."

I nodded, though I had no intention of meeting the priestess. I had no use for their silly stories about dragons and queens. I excused myself, taking Kenwith's hand and fleeing that side of the palace for the comfort of Kenwith's rooms.

My curiosity was stronger than my disbelief, however, drawing me back to the palace library early in the day. The morning sun slanted in through the windows, casting a golden light across the floor as I let myself in, clutching the old book in my hand that I had used as my excuse for coming. There was no movement in the library as I put the book back, no sound that would tell me that Hella-ma had arrived.

I wandered among the shelves, following them back, my eyes scanning over book spines and waiting for one of them to speak to me.

When I had reached volumes that were among the oldest kept in the archives, she appeared soundlessly. "Come."

Her had was light on mine, but somehow it compelled me to follow, further into the dark corners where I had never ventured and to a door that opened into a dark stairwell. Her feet never faltered and somehow, I felt no dread, even as we left the light of the morning behind us.

"Only one of the blood can enter this room." Hella-ma said softly in the dark. "Lift your hand to the door."

She let go of me and I lifted my hand, touching it to the wood. There was the sound of a lock, several of them, then the door swung inward away from my hand. "Step inside."

The room beyond that door was large and round. As I stepped inside, candles and torches lit themselves as if by magic, startling me. The marble floor wore a coat of dust that spoke of the time that had passed since anyone had entered the room. The walls were dark wood, punctuated by marble pillars. Dragons adorned the ceiling.

"What is this place?" I asked, turning back to the door where Hella-ma waited.

"It was once the throne room. It is said that the ceiling can be opened, to allow the dragons who ruled here to fly out."

"I thought you were speaking in metaphors." I said, turning again to take in the room.

"Larun-do was the last to open this room. He could not transform, however."

I snorted before I could stop it. "And you suppose I can?"

"If I am correct." Hella-ma responded. "And I believe I am. But you are not yet ready. There is much for you to learn. If you are willing."

To say I was skeptical, would be an understatement, but the possibility intrigued me enough that I set out on a course of education under the tutelage of the priestess and her sisters. I was sworn to secrecy and whisked off to the temple every morning to be immersed in history that was not taught to the people any more, except as myths and legends.

I learned the truth of the coming of the dragons, of ancestors who stepped up to lead a people on the verge of starvation, building a nation from a collection of tribes. Once stable, the dragons had withdrawn, preferring their lives of quiet in the country beyond the city that they helped to build. More than a century passed before war threatened, as much from within as from without. The dragons returned then, driving out the enemy and setting themselves to lead the people once more.

They were reluctant kings and queens, ancient wisdom guiding them to work toward teaching the people to lead themselves without need of royalty.

The last of them, a queen called Dusha-na, gave birth to ten children before she relinquished the throne, and set them to stay and watch over the people, to aid them and guide them as they progressed in self-governance.

None of it spoke to the idea that the dragons were changlings that lived much of their lives in bodies like mine, or how, exactly, one was to go about transforming. After nearly a whole season of lessons, it was deemed time for me to return to the throne room.

My head was swimming with all of the things I had learned and read as my father escorted me down the stairs. Expectation hung in the air as we gathered near the door and Hella-ma spoke the old language over me. Larun-do opened the door and we stepped inside, bringing the lights to life. I was fairly certain that I still did not believe them as I stepped to the center of the room.

I had no idea what they were expecting to happen. I stood where I had been told to stand and waited.

Nothing happened.

"Speak the words." Hella-ma said from the doorway.

I opened the folded-up paper I had put in my pocket. The words were ancient, a dialect of the old language that I had never seen. Hella-ma had spent many hours teaching me to say them

I held the paper and said the words, feeling foolish. Larun-do stepped to my side and spoke them with me, bolstering my confidence. After three recitations, we fell silent.

Nothing moved, the air itself seemed to still and settle as if waiting with us. My stomach twisted and my hands began to shake. The paper fell from my fingers and everything seemed to change in an instant, my vision narrowing and expanding and my limbs burning.

I screamed, but the sound came out as more of a roar as I dropped to my knees and my back ripped open. Fire burned my stomach and my body contorted as dark blue scales covered my skin, my hands becoming claws with sharp talons. It seemed an eternity passed before it was over, and I was completely changed

My father had fallen back to the door, his mouth dropped open. Beyond the door, Hella-ma and her sisters had fallen to their knees and were busy praying. Exhaustion pulled at me and I could not hold the transformation, collapsing to the marble floor naked and once more a woman.

I remember little of what followed, though it involved Larun-do bundling me in a robe and carrying me up the stairs. For several days, I slept and ate and little more. Kenwith stayed by my side, a comfort to be certain. I had told her little of my studies and nothing of the notion that I might be a dragon. Who would believe such nonsense anyway?

I recovered and found myself ravenous for meat. In the days and nights that followed, I would often find myself in the kitchens, scouring for meat between meals. Hella-ma insisted that it was needed, to feed the dragon within and she encouraged me to try again and again.

With each attempt, the transformation came easier, and I was less drained, even when I held the change for well over an hour. I found the dragon to be empowering. She was strong and fierce when well fed and when I stood tall, stretching out my wings, my head nearly touched the domed ceiling and my wings ended just before the walls.

She filled my dreams with soaring among clouds and rain and I longed for the day when I could leap into the air and follow those dreams out into the world.

That day would come as the Fall began. I was restless and slipped from the bed I shared with Kenwith, tracing the path to the library and down the stairs without need of light. The dragon called to me and I was helpless to resist her. The lights of the fall painted the library in hues of blue and purple and red. The red came only every ten Falls or so, dancing in the skies above the other colors. I dropped my sleeping gown as I entered the throne room, reaching within myself for the fierce fire and calling the dragon to come out.

As the transformation came through me, the roof began to move, the lights of the Fall bathing me, singing to me and without thought, I surrendered myself to the need, leaping into the air and flying free into the night. The sound of the air was musical, and instinctively, I moved my wings, catching the wind and riding it up into the dancing lights. I gave no mind to the houses below me, nor the caution the priestesses had urged upon me.

Nothing could contain me as I embraced the truth of myself and soared through the colors, dancing with them, following them over the hills beyond the city before circling back. I knew I shouldn't exhaust myself, so reluctantly I returned to that open roof, settling down to the marble floor, my wings folding inward as my talons clacked against the stone.

I did not see Kenwith at the door, but I heard her sharp intake of air and turned, even as the transformation reversed and my body returned to that of a woman. I reached out a hand as if to comfort her, but she turned and ran up the stairs. I tried to follow, but the flight had drained me and it was all I could do to pull my sleeping gown back onto my body.

I rested there, at the door until I had the strength to climb the stairs. I returned to Kenwith's suite to find the door locked. I sank to the floor beside it, wanting to tell her to not be afraid, wishing I had told her more about what was happening to me. The door didn't open until morning, and when it did, Kenwith looked startled to find me there.

"Kenwith." I stood, one hand holding the wall for support. "Let me explain."

She shook her head. "No, Chenna. I know what I saw."

"I have not changed." Which was a lie, I knew. I had changed. I was still changing.

"Is this why you came here?"

I shook my head. "No. I only wanted to know where my mother came from."

"Then maybe it's time that you leave." Kenwith said. "If the houses of congress were to find out what you are..."

"I will hide it, I will never change again."

She shook her head. "You cannot deny what you are, Chenna."

"Please, Kenwith. I did not want this. I never wanted..." But I did want it now, now that I had felt the euphoria that came with taking wing. My whole body craved it.

"I have a charity meeting with my mother." Kenwith said, turning on her heel and stalking away. She left the door open for me to go in. I bathed and dressed in the most modest clothes I could find, sitting myself at her vanity to brush through my dark hair. The colors of my skin seemed to be brighter, more intense.

I found myself wondering how I appeared as a dragon. I was still sitting at the vanity when there was a knock on the door and Hella-ma entered the room. "We must take you to the temple," she said urgently. "Before you are discovered."

"I don't understand." I let her tug me to my feet and toward the door.

"We have been exposed," she responded. "The Counsel of Commons has issued a summons to have you brought before them."

I frowned as she bustled me through corridors and out to a doorway that led to an external doorway near one of the bridges open to the public. One of her sisters met us there, draping me in one of their red robes and hustling me toward the bridge. I drew the deep hood up over my head as we stepped onto the bridge. It was the time of the Fall, the only time these bridges were empty. I kept my head down as we walked, trying to slow the rapid burning inside of me that longed to take to the skies.

Hella-ma whispered directions, and I followed because I didn't know what else to do. The Counsel of Commons was the largest house of the congress, and the one who most often dealt out punishment for broken laws. I had not broken any laws that I could place. My mind skipped to Kenwith, and the fear I had seen in her eyes.

Surely, she would not have gone to the Counsel of Commons. She would have taken her fear to her father, who sat on the Counsel of Lords. The thought came to me that perhaps she had, and he, in turn had gone to the Counsel of Commons.

I was still thinking about that when we reached the shadows of the red temple that was nearly as old as the palace itself. I was ushered into the quiet, into the sanctuary where I at last felt safe enough to push back the hood of my robe. My father was there, and with him several aids and others I had seen at various times.

"Are you okay?" Larun-do asked as he approached me.

"I am uncertain." I said. "What happened?"

He lifted an eyebrow at me. "You went flying last night."

I frowned, crossing my arms. "It is the Fall. No one saw me, save Kenwith, who must have followed me. She saw me return."

"I saw you, but then, I was out in the garden. When I heard you'd been summoned, I assumed you were seen by someone else."

"If she was, whomever raised the alarm would have to answer for why they were out on a night in the Fall." Hella-ma said.

"So, we must assume that one of the servants overheard something." Larun-do said, one hand on my shoulder. "We must decide our next course of action."

"Action?" I shook my head. "You had a plan, didn't you? There was a reason you have not publicly claimed me, a reason why we were keeping this entire thing a secret?"

"There was. There is. But we are not ready yet."

"Maybe it's time you fill me in on this plan."

They had kept me in the dark for the most part, teaching me the history and language enough that I could find the dragon within, but I still had no idea what they were planning beyond that.

"We are working with a group of people that are tired of the corruption within the Counsels." Larun-do said. "We had hoped that once you had manifested your true nature we could have you reclaim the throne our ancestors abandoned and wipe the slate clean."

"You. . . ." The notion of it swam around inside me. They had made me a traitor without even allowing me to know the full weight of their plans. Though looking back now, I must confess that on some level I knew this was why they had been tutoring me.

The dragon within longed to come to life, to eliminate the threats that now faced us.

"We are safe enough until the end of the Fall." Hella-ma said.

"Maybe we should act now, while they cower away from the lights." Larun-do countered. "Set loose the dragon to clear out the palace."

"What is it you would have me do, Father?" I asked, my voice displaying my displeasure. "Shall I burn it to the ground? Kill all of those within? How would that serve anything but destruction?"

"No, of course not," he replied. "Unless there is no other way."

I turned away in disgust, my stomach growling its emptiness. "I require food." I said. "I have not eaten since my transformation last night."

I said nothing else until the food was brought to me. I sat with my back to them and ate, my thoughts churning. They would not move against us during the Fall, nor would they violate the sanctuary.

I underestimated the fear of those who would lose power if the people were to know that the dragons had returned. I had sated the need within me for sustenance, and was pondering the wisdom of merely taking wing and leaving all together when the sound of doors being broken open roused me from my contemplations.

Larun-do, jumped to my side, determined to protect me I suppose, as the sanctuary filled with armed men. The fighting was brief, the temple's priestesses overwhelmed by sheer numbers.

I was dragged from behind my father, my arms pinned behind my back, a heavy collar put on my neck, forcing me to my knees. The man who seemed to be in charge stepped up beside me, his weapon under my chin pulling my face up.

"You don't look much like a dragon," he sneered.

I wanted to prove him wrong, but even with the meat warming my belly, I did not think I could transform with the heavy iron restraints holding me. "Really, Larun-do, I would have thought you would be more protective of your little plot."

My father was forced to his knees beside me. "And I would have expected better of you too, Kava."

I blinked at the man who now held us prisoner. Kava, the head of the Counsel of Lords. "No matter, we have all the proof we need. Trial will commence in two days, when the Fall has ended.

We were dragged from the temple and separated, and I was taken up into this tiny tower room where even now I await my fate. There is no hope of fleeing now, even if there were room enough to transform. I am surrounded by stone and iron. All I have of freedom is the view out my window as the lights dance along the sky.

If this were a fairy story, the kind we tell children as we put them to bed, there would be some happy ending. Kenwith would come to release me, and we would win the day. But this is not a fairy tale, and Kenwith has not come to even see me since my arrest. In the morning there will be a trial, by tomorrow evening, I expect I shall be dead.

The fire burns within me, but I shall never again taste the euphoria of flight, and when I am gone there will be dragons no more.

The End

About the Author: Natalie J Case

An avid reader from a very early age, Natalie grew up in worlds that only exist in books. Her influences run the gamut of genres, from childhood mysteries like Nancy Drew and The Bobsey Twins to epic fantasy and hardcore sci-fi.

Jericho Jordan is an introduction to a character and story that will likely come to fruition sometime in 2018. Currently, she is working on the second series in the *Shades and Shadows* series, a set of paranormal thrillers. The first in that series, *Through Shade and Shadow* was released in 2017.

Books by Natalie J Case:
Forever
Through Shade and Shadow

Links:
Facebook: https://www.facebook.com/authornataliejcase/
Twitter: http://twitter.com/nataliejcase
Website: https://nataliejcase.com/

Tenelach: Legends of the Tri-Gard Vol. 1.5

By Michelle Lynn

Chapter One

To look upon the village was to see heartbreak. Yet, Mira couldn't look away. It was her home. These people were supposed to be her family, her friends, and they were starving. It was hard to feel anything at all for them but pity. She looked up from her place near the hearth to examine her mother's fine bones, sharp and gaunt. The skin was loose over her frame.

As a child, Mira could remember her mother as a plump woman with rosy cheeks. The years had changed them all.

Her father was still the looming figure of her youth, but there was a resignation in him that was painful to see.

Mira held out her hands to let the fire thaw the ice in her veins.

Twenty years to the day. That was how long it had been since magic ran through their lands. She'd been seven when it was stolen and the entire realm of Dreach-Sciene began its downward spiral into ruin. Seven was old enough to remember; old enough to wish she could forget.

There'd been such joy. It was a kind of joy that only an intense connection to the earth could bring. Without magic, that connection was lost.

In the village, they called her a spinster and maybe that was what she was.

Her face still held much of the beauty that others had lost through the hard years. Wide golden eyes sat deep in a face that was framed with thick honey curls. She was thin – as they all were – but managed to hold on to a few of her curves.

The men in the village desired her, but she had yet to meet someone who could challenge her. She didn't want to be only a wife or a mother. She didn't know what she wanted.

Except that more than anything she longed to fall in love.

"I'm going to go into the forest to find some berries," she said, getting to her feet.

Her mother looked up suddenly. "Mira," she sneered. "It is too cold." What her mother really meant was that looking for berries was a useless task because they had long depleted that resource.

Mira looked back at where her mother was stirring the large pot of potato stew that sat over the fire. It wouldn't be enough to keep her brother and sister from crying out with hunger in the night. Hanging her head low, she fastened a cloak about her shoulders and stepped out into the evening chill with a basket swinging from her arm.

The sound of running feet drifted in the air and she turned just in time to catch her brother as he ran past. Toro laughed as she lifted his small frame. Their sister Tara crashed into them from behind and wrapped her arms around Mira's legs.

Such laughter seemed like it didn't belong in their village. People stared as Mira squeezed her siblings. They were only eight. They didn't yet know there was nothing to smile about in their lives.

"Can we come into the forest, Mira?" Toro asked.

"Please?" Tara jumped up and down.

Mira set Toro back on his feet and leaned down to look at the both of them. "Not today, I'm afraid."

"Oooo," Toro looked at Tara. "She wants to be alone."

The little girl crossed her arms over her chest. "She always wants to be alone."

Mira had nothing to say to that so she ushered them inside and then took off down the path through the village. People stared as she went by, but that was nothing new. They called her odd and didn't speak to her.

She didn't mind. She preferred books to people anyways. Maybe that was the problem. She glanced down at the book of stories hidden in her basket. Books were a rare and precious commodity. An old woman in the village had given this one to her before she died and it was Mira's most valued possession. She wouldn't be able to read in the waning light, but having it with her made her believe in the impossible again.

Her life was no fairy-tale. She had yet to meet a man she would consider princely. Magic no longer existed in their land. She didn't believe in happily-ever-afters. All she had was trying to survive.

Before the wars that ended in the destruction of magic, life had been simple. It had been good. She'd had a good childhood. Then the fighting came. It reached every corner of their realm. No one was safe. No one was spared. Her own father was injured. Their king was killed and their lives were forever changed.

The path she trod took her away from the village towards the large expanse of trees that stretched as far as she could see. If she kept walking, she knew that in maybe a week's time, she would reach the shores of whitecap and the sea of Uisce that could take her to the lands beyond. Maybe there was something better out there, something more.

Her legs tired more quickly than she wished and she realized that getting away from her village was only a fantasy. She couldn't remember the last time she'd had the energy to make it past the edge of the trees. It was probably the last time her belly was full.

She set her basket down and dropped to her knees beside a large oak tree. Its branches were twisted and held their dead leaves hanging above her head. She looked up as one drifted down to land on her shoulder. Her fingers picked up the dried, brown leaf and crushed it between them.

A tear leaked from her eye at the thought that this was the only way her brother and sister knew the forest. To them, it was dark and dead. In her mind, it still held so much life. Little feet used to run through the wildflowers, picking them for her mother.

Little mouths used to munch on berries as bright red juice dripped down their chins.

The wind whipped up around her, willing her to go home to warm herself by her fire.

She refused.

Only yesterday, it had been too hot to cook in their small house. Without magic to keep the world in balance, nothing made sense.

She would not bow down to hopelessness.

As if called, she leaned forward and placed her palms on the ground in front of her. Her dress bunched and she shifted her skirts to kick her legs free. Her curls had fallen loose and hung forward as she closed her eyes.

She could hear it.

She always did.

The low hum echoed off the trees surrounding her, a vibration trailing up her arms. It was the only time she felt strong, hopeful – when she was connecting in this way.

After the magic was gone, she'd discovered her connection to the earth. It had taken her years to realize what it was. Her people called it the Tenelach. She could literally hear the earth sing. She could feel it in every bone.

Only it wasn't supposed to exist. Tenelach was a myth. It was said to be a deeper connection than magic had provided and therefor it could not be. When she'd first told her parents, they thought it was a child's fantasies. Then they started to tell her to grow up and to forget what she thought she knew. That was the day they began to see her as more of a burden than a beloved child.

The people were angry. She hadn't seen it at the time, but now it was plain. Losing their magic was like losing everything they knew. They didn't know how else to live. It left them empty and feeling so very alone. They didn't want to believe there were those who didn't have to feel that.

So she stopped talking about it.

Lifting her face to the sky, she kept her eyes squeezed shut and began humming in time with the earth. Her hums turned into words and before long, she found herself singing. Her pure voice rang out and she would have sworn she felt a surge of joy rush up her arms from the ground below.

A smile curved her lips and she continued, lost in a world that no one else would ever understand.

* * *

Wren had come a long way since day break. It was all he could do to stay in his saddle, but the images continued to run through his mind. Three days ago, he'd come across a supply train from Dreach-Dhoun that was traveling to the Duke's estate in Isenore.

Wren's father was a noble who served Isenore faithfully, but he'd always said his first loyalty was to the king. Dreach-Sciene contained three kingdoms

– Isenore, Aldorwood, and the Isle of Sona. That was what he knew. The king was their leader and he would never sell them out to their enemies. Dreach-Dhoun was the enemy.

At his father's urgings, Wren had left Isenore behind. Lord Eisner, the duke, would call upon his nobles soon. They'd be expected to provide soldiers. Wren was his father's greatest fighter. He was considered the greatest fighter in Isenore. That was why he had to leave his home. He would only fight for his king.

The roads had become dangerous and the villages suspicious. He knew stopping was not a good idea. He barely glanced at the village as he rode passed. He'd enter the forest and take the paths the rest of the way to the palace. Once he reached the trees, he could rest for the night.

His horse needed rest as well. He'd ridden him hard. They entered the forest at a slow gait. When a woman's voice reached his ears, he pulled up on the reins and looked around. It was getting dark and the woods were no place for a woman at night.

He rode towards the sound and stopped when he saw her. The breath rushed out of his lungs.

A beautiful woman was kneeling on the forest floor, her dress was bunched up to reveal long legs. He knew he should look away, but he couldn't. Her blonde hair hung wild, almost feral, as she flung her head back. Her eyes were closed and her lips parted to release a mesmerizing song.

He jerked in his saddle and his horse stepped back, snapping a twig in the process.

The singing ceased abruptly and the woman's eyes snapped open. She looked at him for a long moment as if she knew not what to do. Then she stood so abruptly that it spooked his horse.

The brown stallion reared back suddenly. Wren wasn't prepared and a strangled cry rose up from his throat. He held on to his saddle with all his strength, but the horse stepped backwards and reared again. Before he knew it was happening, he was falling free of his beast.

His body slammed into the ground and the horse's hoof caught him in the stomach. The sounds around him faded away and his vision went in and out.

The girls face appeared before his. Her lips moved, but he heard nothing.

Blackness tugged at the corners of his vision before finally pulling him under its thick veil.

Mira stared on in shock. Finding a man watching her when she was in the midst of her connection was like having a bucket of cold water flung on her. She'd been so stunned, she'd spooked his horse.

The beast stopped its tantrum when she made no further threatening moves and now it approached her cautiously.

She glanced from the horse to the now motionless man and her wits came back to her. She rushed forward.

"Are you okay?" she asked, crouching down.

No response. Not even a groan.

She thought furiously, trying to remember what to do. Her father was the town healer, but without magic or even fresh herbs, that consisted mainly of setting bones and sewing cuts.

Then it came to her. She pressed a finger into his neck just as her father had shown her. The strong thumps against it was proof of life.

She sat back on her heels, her chest heaving. "Oh, thank the earth. You aren't dead."

She didn't know what to do. The people of the village would tell her to leave him and take his horse. He would only be one more mouth to feed.

But that was why she was different than them.

She tugged at his arm to roll him over, realizing there was no way she could get him back to her father. Her eyes scanned the forest around them. It was as good a place as any. Most would tell her the woods were dangerous, but she felt safer there than she did back in town.

She knew how to survive on her own. She thought of the potato soup her mom had been making back home. If she didn't return, there might be enough to keep the pangs at bay for her brother and sister. It wasn't the first time she'd gone without food and it wouldn't be the last.

But the night was cold and it was getting dark. Mira looked at the man once more and noticed the shining sword hanging at his belt. She slid it carefully from its scabbard and went in search of firewood, sword in hand for protection. Everything was so dry, that wouldn't be hard.

Before long, she had a fire going. She pushed the man closer to it and then settled back against a tree. Examining the sword in her hand more closely, she noticed the quality. Blades like this did not belong among the villages in Dreach-Sciene. She wondered who he was.

For the first time, she also wondered if she should be frightened of him. The fire lit up his face in an orange glow. He was young, probably near her own age, and handsome – she couldn't deny that. His dark hair was long and tied back away from his face. She found herself wishing she could see the color of his eyes.

She watched his chest rise and fall and felt an unwelcome gratitude rise up. Mira didn't want to be happy for the excuse to avoid home. She wished more than anything to find her place there. Her eyes found a far-off point and she knew that would never happen. She would never belong there. She was meant for more.

Her eyes were beginning to drift shut, when the man started to cough. She looked towards him and found his eyes on her. She didn't know how long he'd been staring. Reaching her arms up, she pushed her hair back and tried to tame it as best she could. She had already appeared wild to this unknown man.

The man wheezed and gripped his side.

"Are you in pain?" Mira asked.

He didn't answer her, but his eyes held the truth. "You stayed." He tried to push himself up, but didn't have the strength and ended up falling back with a frustrated grunt.

She looked on in worry and a tiny bit of amusement.

"I'd stay still if I were you."

His eyes assessed her and she squirmed under his gaze. It had been a while since anyone looked at her with anything other than scorn or pity. In this man's eyes, all she saw was curiosity.

"You're holding my sword," he stated calmly.

"I am." She ran a hand down the blade.

"Can I have it back?" He reached out, expecting her to pass it to him.

"No."

He narrowed his eyes. "A soldier's sword is an extension of oneself. You shouldn't be handling it."

"Are you a soldier?"

"Yes."

"Because this blade is too good for that of a simple soldier."

"You see much, my lady." Suspicion entered his voice.

"What else is one to do with their eyes?" She laughed at him and he flushed. He tried to sit up again and this time succeeded.

"How badly are you hurt?" Her face grew serious.

"Nothing I haven't felt before."

"Don't be such a man," she snapped. "I'm trying to ascertain if I can get you to my father for healing."

"I don't need to see a healer. I must be on my way."

She huffed in annoyance. "Like you could even get into your saddle right now." She moved closer. "What's your name?"

His lips curved up into the most charming smile she'd ever seen and he stuck out his hand. "Wren. It's a pleasure to meet you ..."

"Mira," she finished for him, clasping his hand.

Warmth sizzled up her arm and her breath caught in her throat. Wren's eyes held an intensity that ensnared her gaze. She couldn't look away. His grip on her hand tightened until she almost couldn't feel anything at all.

"Mira." His lips caressed her name, testing it out on his tongue.

The sound of her name jolted her back to herself and she released him and jumped away. Getting to her feet, she straightened out the bottom of her dress.

"I don't have any food," she finally said. "I must return to the village."

"It is late," he responded. "Why didn't you just go through my saddle bags?"

"Why would I? They do not belong to me."

"There is food enough in there so you have no reason to return this night."

She hugged her arms across her chest. "I don't know you, sir. I am certainly not going to spend all night in the woods with you."

"You had no problem doing so when you thought I was unconscious. Surely it is safer with me awake."

"How do I know you aren't what I need protecting from?"

He grinned. "You're a smart woman."

"That surprises you?" There was no offense in her voice, only curiosity.

"No. It ... pleases me."

"Then tell me why you travel these woods alone. Why am I not to fear you?"

He leaned back with a sigh. "I come from Isenore to join the king's forces as we prepare for war."

Her face scrunched in distaste at the mention of Isenore. The Lord Eisner was almost as hated as King Calis of Dreach-Dhoun. He didn't come out as evil blatantly, but people saw beneath the surface. He was not a good man.

Wren moved around to get more comfortable and Mira found herself intrigued by him. He was so very different than every man she'd known in her life. His body was not beaten down by a life of hard work. His soul was not crushed by the hopelessness perpetuated inside the village. There was still a brightness to his eyes rather than a dull acceptance of one's fate. When he laughed, it was like music, finally breaking through into a world with no sound.

Her life had been so utterly devoid of laughter.

"I don't want to go back," she finally admitted. "At least not tonight. But don't try to kill me." It was her first attempt at a joke in a very long time and silence followed it. She closed her eyes for the briefest of moments, opening them when Wren's soft chuckling reached her ears. She leaned back with a satisfied smile.

Chapter Two

Wren was not immune to the charms of a beautiful woman. He was the son of a noble – a minor noble, but still – so he was constantly surrounded by women whose hair, makeup, and dress were so done up that they couldn't be anything other than beautiful.

The woman across from him had no charms to speak of. She tried to joke and it seemed so unnatural coming out of her that he couldn't help but laugh. Her blonde curls were wild and untamed. Her rosy cheeks were unpainted. She wore a dress that had definitely seen better days.

She was a commoner. His court would look down on women like her. They would say she was not worthy, that she had no smarts; no beauty.

And they would be wrong. Her calculating eyes held more knowledge in them than he could imagine. Her undone look was endearing.

She'd helped him when most would have left him for dead. There was a time when that wasn't true. When he was a child, Dreach-Sciene had been a place where the people looked out for each other. There were plenty of resources to go around so they could afford to.

Now, helping a stranger meant giving a little bit of what you had. It meant putting someone else above yourself. That was not something that people could afford to do anymore. Heck, he wasn't sure he'd stop for a stranger.

She'd done it without a second thought. Or at least, he assumed it was without a second thought because he'd been unconscious.

He watched her as she tentatively rummaged in his pack, her eyes going wide. His father had insisted he take plenty of food. They were on rations, but his father wanted him to be taken care of. He knew it meant his father would be going without enough food this week.

It shamed him to accept it, but it would have shamed the old man more had he refused.

Mira pulled out a hunk of cheese and broke it in two. She took the much smaller part and tossed the other to him. She didn't touch the bread or ale.

Food in hand, she sat back down next to where she'd laid his sword. He doubted she even knew how to use the thing.

He took a bite, hoping it would give him some much-needed strength. His ribs hurt and his head was worse, but all he needed was a night's sleep and he'd be back on the road. It was important to his father that he join in this fight, so it was important to him.

The truth was that his father had suspicions about the duke they served. He didn't trust his loyalty and if Lord Eisner switched sides in the wars to come, then many of his nobles would as well. Not Wren's family though. Their loyalty would always be to the king and he took pride in that fact.

Across the fire, he saw Mira shiver. "We can use the horse's blanket." He pointed to where Mira had unsaddled the horse and left the blanket nearby.

She didn't respond and he knew why.

"It's cold out here," he urged. "And that's the only blanket we've got."

She stared at him – or through him.

"You know what? You can just use it. Don't worry about me." He huffed an impatient sigh. He wasn't used to sleeping on the ground or in the cold. His warm, feather bed at home sounded very good right about then.

Mira finally stood, her movements stiff. She walked towards the saddle and moved it out of the way to lift the heavy blanket. Her nose wrinkled at the smell and he almost laughed. She joined him on his side of the fire and threw the blanket down before lowering herself to the ground.

"I don't know you," she said. "I still think you might kill me." She put up a hand to stop his protests. "But I'd really rather not freeze to death in the night."

"You could just leave me here and go home to your warm, inviting home."

She looked away and he sensed a hesitancy there so he didn't press her about her home. Instead, he spread the blanket across their laps, enjoying the warm cocoon it created. She was so close he could feel her movements. She smelled of earth, raw and fresh. A breeze whipped through their clearing, rustling the dried leaves along the ground and fanning Mira's hair out behind her.

She burrowed further into the warmth of the blanket, pulling it up to her chin.

He remembered how she looked when he first found her. She'd looked so peaceful yet so powerful all at once. It was mesmerizing. He knew he should be on his way to the palace, but he couldn't bring himself to regret being there in that moment.

It was the Tenelach. He knew it the moment he saw it. He'd only ever known one person who claimed to have had it. When he was a child, there was an older woman in his father's household. He'd been fascinated because she could do things with her magic that no one else could. Then the magic was drained and she turned into nothing more than a sad old woman mourning the past. She died only a few years later and he had thought the Tenelach was no longer possible without that power.

But he saw it with his own eyes. She'd been connected to the earth in a way he hadn't seen since the war. It was part of her – this wild woman.

He felt her body nudge closer to his and looked over. She was asleep, her face relaxed for the first time since he'd met her. She was no longer on guard. He let her press up against his side and closed his eyes.

The blanket fell from around her, but she was still warm beside him, only confirming his suspicions.

Yes. The Tenelach.

* * *

Wren woke slowly, cracking his eyes open to let in the blinding sunlight. The warm presence he'd felt all night was gone and a panic suddenly overtook him. Did she leave? He couldn't bear the thought of never seeing her again.

He managed to sit up, the pain still there from the day before. It had lessened, but he worried riding would still be out of the question.

His eyes scanned the area around them, finally landing on Mira's form. She had her back leaning against a tree and a book sat open in her lap.

"You can read?" He hadn't meant to sound so surprised.

She jerked her head up and snapped the book shut. "That's none of your business."

"I'm ... I'm sorry. It's just that most of the commoners in Isenore can't read, especially the women." He cringed as he replayed those words in his head. He'd just insulted her and had no way of taking it back.

She climbed to her feet and brushed off her dress before putting the book in her basket. "How are you feeling?" Her voice held no emotion and he knew after that comment she just wanted to get rid of him.

"I should be on my way." He managed to climb to his feet and walk towards the saddle. His body screamed as he tried to lift it and he let out a growl as it slid from his grasp and landed on the ground with a soft thud.

Without a word, Mira walked up beside him and lifted the saddle. She was stronger than she looked. She managed to get it on the horse and buckle it.

Wren looked on, ashamed at his own weakness.

"I could have gotten that," he said.

"Fool," she snapped. "You aren't riding off on your own if you can't even saddle your horse. Think you can ride if I help you?"

He kicked at the dirt. "Probably."

"Good. Now that you can stand, we're taking you to my father."

Without another word, she motioned him over. It took many tries, but they finally managed to get him onto the horse. She climbed up in front of him.

The woman was full of surprises.

"Hold on," she said, taking the reins in her hands.

He scooted closer and wrapped an arm around her waist. Her hair hit him in the face so he brushed it over one shoulder, his fingertips skimming her skin. She gave the horse a small kick and when it took off, she moved against him.

He closed his eyes, enjoying her feel even as his body ached for him to stop moving. A blinding pain was starting behind his right eye and his head lulled forward. When his chin landed on Mira's shoulder, she used her free hand to grip the arm he had around her.

They trotted over open land and it wasn't long before they were on the streets of the small village.

Wren felt eyes on them as their horse walked by, unfriendly eyes. He caught quite a few people throwing their sneers Mira's way and it made an anger rise up inside of him. He'd only known her for a single day, but he knew she didn't deserve the way they looked at her.

Their looks turned from scorn to curiosity and a little suspicion when they traveled from her to him.

"Do you think you can get down on your own?" she asked, seemingly unaffected by the attitudes of her neighbors.

"I can try."

She gave his arm a squeeze before stopping outside a small home and sliding down. Immediately a thin woman appeared at the door.

"Where on this earth have you been, Mira?" Her voice had a screeching quality that only made Wren's headache worse. "I needed you to help with the twins and there are chores that need doing."

"Thank you for your worry, mother. I'm fine."

"Don't you sass me."

Their argument was broken up by a crash from behind as Wren attempted to slide down from the horse and ended up in a pile on the ground.

"Wren!" Mira screamed, rushing to his side. She bent down and looked into his glazed eyes then glanced back at her mother. "Where's father?"

"I'm here," he said, stepping from the house. "What trouble have you brought to us this time, Mira?"

A crowd of neighbors had gathered. Mira knew her father would be angry, but she also knew he would not turn away someone who needed help.

"This is Wren. I found him in the woods. He was on his way to join the king's forces when he got injured."

Her father sighed. "Garrick," he called. A man appeared from the crowd. "Take the horse somewhere where no one will think about turning him into food."

The horse was led away and Wren's foggy mind couldn't grasp that things were so desperate for that to even be a consideration. He glanced at Mira, painfully away that she'd probably made it worse by bringing him to her home.

Mira's father walked forward and leaned down to haul Wren to his feet. "Sir," Wren said, trying to walk on his own. "I'd like to thank you in advance for your help."

"Thank my daughter." He scowled. "She's the idiot of the family."

Mira blushed furiously and hung her head in embarrassment. Wren wanted nothing more than to tell her parents how wrong they were, but in that moment, the fog in his mind grew thicker. As soon as he was led to a bed, he collapsed into unconsciousness.

Chapter Three

The long day passed and he hadn't woken. They ate their meager food and went about their daily chores all while a stranger lay sprawled on one of the beds. Only, he didn't feel like a stranger to Mira. She watched his face as soft snores sounded in her ears and knew there was something different about him.

She thought about the extra food in his saddle bags for just a moment and glanced at her brother and sister. No, she couldn't steal from this man.

He'd left his home to join the army that the king would surely be calling upon soon. When she was in the midst of her connection with the earth, she could feel something large happening. It was as if the very ground held a suppressed joy that it covered with trepidation. What was coming was going to have monumental consequences.

Her eyes scanned the room. Would it change all of this? Would it allow her to be free? Her fingers tingled in remembrance of a time when magic flowed freely from the land. She sighed loudly. She'd do anything to feel in running through her veins again.

But she wasn't doing anything.

This man from Isenore was giving up everything. He had a lot to lose. She had nothing and yet here she sat as the realm prepared.

The room was lit only by a ring of candles and the fire that burned in the stove. Her mother and father's shadowed figures huddled around the stove for warmth. Her siblings had long gone to bed on their small pallets. The silence made her smile. It wasn't often she got a moment of peace.

Wren mumbled something in his sleep and Mira grasped one of the candles and moved closer. The flame cast his face in light.

Rustling came from behind her and she noticed her parents putting out the fire and crawling under their tattered blankets. She listened for a few minutes before she heard her father's snoring and her mother's even breaths.

The one room house was full of people, but she could still feel so alone.

Wren had been placed on her bed so she knew she was in for a cold and dirty night on the ground. It didn't make her eager for sleep.

Wren's pink lips moved slowly as if he would speak. Strain appeared in the fine lines of his handsome face and he jerked his head from side to side.

"No," he mumbled. "No."

She laid a hand on his shoulder and felt his entire body quiver. Tears appeared at the corners of his still closed eyes.

"Please, Zak."

His chest convulsed and fear bloomed in her chest. After checking him over, her father had told her he would be fine with some rest, but she'd wondered if he just didn't want to use any of their limited supplies on a stranger.

"Wren," she whispered. "Wren, wake up."

His eyes shot open and he stared at her for a tense moment before recognition took hold. His gaze darted around the room as he struggled to catch his breath.

He eventually relaxed and she realized her hand was still on his shoulder.

"Sorry." She pulled it away quickly.

He shot her a weak smile and ran a hand through his sweaty hair. "How long have I been out?"

"Just today. My father said you needed rest and then could be on your way."

"I don't want to be a burden on your family. You've been so kind."

"You're not," she stammered then stopped herself and sighed. "Okay, maybe you are, but you needed help. What kind of person would I be if I didn't do what I can."

His eyes widened in wonder. "I've never met anyone like you before."

She laughed nervously. "You mean an odd girl with nothing better to do than look for stray men in the woods?"

He reached out boldly and took the hand she'd placed on the bed beside him. "Kind. Beautiful. I've seen a lot of this realm. Trust me when I tell you that you are as rare as they come. Distrust, anger, and selfishness have become a way of life in Dreach-Sciene."

"They've had to. It's how people survive."

"Then tell me, how do you survive?"

She pulled her hand away and looked away. "Surviving is easy because we have no choice. It's living that's difficult."

"Aren't those the same thing?"

"No." She fiddled with the ends of her hair. "They're not. Excuse me. I must get some sleep."

"Oh, but I must be in your bed." He tried to sit up. "I can take the floor."

"You absolutely cannot!"

"My lady Mira, you cannot sleep on the ground."

"Of course I can. I'm not the one who let my horse step on me."

He tried to get out of the bed, but his strength would not let him and she wasn't inclined to help. A tiny smile played on her lips, but it fell quickly as she curled up on the cold dirt floor. There were no blankets to spare and a shiver ran down her spine. It had grown very cold and she could feel it in her very bones.

Pulling her arms in closer around herself, she laid her head against the dirt. It didn't happen instantly, but her icy limbs began to thaw as a warmth pulsed through her. Placing a palm against the ground, she smiled.

"Thank you," she whispered before falling into a comfortable sleep.

"Get up, Mira."

Mira didn't know how long she'd been asleep before she heard her mother's harsh words and felt the toe of a boot poke into her arm.

"Mira," her mother snapped again.

With a groan, she uncurled herself. Light was just beginning to push away the darkness. It was early.

As soon as she broke her connection and clambered to her feet, the warmth of the night left her.

Her mother scrutinized her. "You need to bathe today."

"Why?"

"Just do as you're told for once in your life, child." She shook her head. "I'll be giving your breakfast portion to our guest." She shot a disgusted look over Mira's shoulder at Wren and left the house.

Her father was already out, presumably with the twins in tow, leaving Mira alone with Wren. She turned to find him sitting up in bed. His lips curved into a smile and she felt a flutter deep in her belly.

Shaking off the feeling, she walked towards the door. "I have to do as she ordered." She grabbed a bucket and ducked out of the house, making her way to the well at the center of town. Each family only got an allotment of water for their daily needs. If her mother was using some on Mira, there must be a reason.

She pumped a generous amount into the bucket, wanting to take advantage of the order. Hefting the heavy bucket, she returned to her home.

"Do you think you can get out of bed?" she asked Wren. Water sloshed over the side of the bucket as she set it down.

He pushed himself up seemingly pleased with the return of some of his strength. Without a word, he swung his legs over the side of the tiny bed and stood. He wobbled slight and then righted himself. "I'll go sit outside the door," he said.

When he was gone, Mira found a sponge and a tiny bit of soap. It had been a good batch she'd made last month and smelled of a flower she didn't know the name of. Flowers of any kind were rare and she'd been amazed to find a small patch of them in the woods.

Undoing the laces of her dress, she pushed it down and stepped out of it as it pooled at her feet. The cool air hit her pale skin and she sucked in a breath.

"I don't envy you," Wren said from the other side of the door.

"I don't know what you're talking about."

"It must be freezing."

Her teeth chattered as she began to sponge her long arms. "It's fine."

"Sure." He chuckled lightly.

She scrubbed her thin legs and then came to the point she'd been dreading. Steeling herself against the oncoming cold, she bent over the bucket and pushed her long hair into the water.

A hissed escaped her lips as she scrubbed it, rinsed it, and flung it back. Icy water trailed down her back.

Wren laughed louder this time.

"I don't know what you find so funny," she snapped.

"I'm just picturing you naked right now."

She stopped moving as his words shocked her brain. Bold didn't even begin to describe them. She should have been angry at his forwardness, but she found she was angry at something else instead.

"And that makes you laugh?" she snapped.

"No, I'm laughing because I imagined your face when I told you that."

She hurriedly pulled on her underclothes and then her dress, leaving the laces slightly undone before marching to the door and yanking it open.

"You're ..." she started. "You're ..."

He climbed to his feet with a flash of pain crossing his face before grinning. "Handsome? I'll bet you were about to say handsome."

"Ugh, I think I liked you better when you were in too much pain to be yourself."

"That hurts, my lady." He held a hand over his heart.

"I'm no lady."

He cocked his head, considering her. "No. You're not, are you?" He stuck his hand into his pocket. "Anyway, I saved you this."

Mira looked down at the bread he'd pulled out and her stomach rumbled at the thought of having even the tiniest bit of food.

"Don't you need that to regain your strength?" she asked.

"I never wanted to take anything from you." He pressed it into her hand. "Here. You must be starving. I would have saved the cheese your mother gave me, but she stared until I ate it. I'm fine. I can just go get the food from my saddle bags."

"Not until you leave. If anyone sees you, they'll take it all."

"Stop worrying about me. Are you going to eat?" As soon as the first crumb passed her lips, she couldn't help herself. She shoved it in hurriedly, sighing as the picked the last crumbs from her hands. "Thank you."

He bowed slightly. "I guess that means I'm forgiven for picturing you naked?"

A laugh burst free of her. "Come back inside. You must be freezing. I'll make us some tea. My mother won't notice a few missing leaves."

He followed her in and watched as she put the water on to boil and pulled her curls over one shoulder, running her fingers through them to smooth out the wet mane. She stared absently into the fire and didn't notice Wren walk up behind her.

She jumped when she felt his cold hand on her back. "Need help with the laces?"

"My mother usually does that. She complains, but she still helps."

Her dress tightened as his nimble fingers worked the laces, occasionally brushing against her skin.

"I have three sisters," he said quietly. "I've done this a time or two."

When he was finished, she spun around to find her face to face with the man who was still very much the stranger. She knew the village would talk if anyone saw that they were alone.

His breath warmed her face and she couldn't decipher the look in his eyes. It was curiosity mixed with something else.

"You have sisters?" she stammered, stepped back to give herself space.

He chuckled briefly and scratched the back of his head. "Three sisters, two brothers."

"Why are you the only one your father sent to the king?"

"As far as I know, the king isn't sending children to war. One of my brothers is so young he barely knows which end of the sword to hold."

"You said you had two."

"Zak ..." A tortured look crossed his face.

"You were calling out to him in your sleep."

He looked embarrassed as he breathed deeply. "I don't know why I'm even telling you this." He sighed. "Zak was kidnapped by a squadron of men from Dreach-Dhoun. They like to take the sons of Isenore nobles to their dungeons and then return their bodies."

Mira reached out and grabbed his arm, sliding her hand down to intertwine her fingers with his. "Wren."

He closed his eyes for a brief moment. "It was a few years ago. Can we talk about something else?"

"Why aren't your sisters with you?"

"Why would my father send them?"

"You don't think women should fight in this war? That's ridiculous. It is just as much our realm as yours. Our bellies are just as empty as any man's. Our lands just as destroyed. I can remember the feel of having magic right at my fingertips, why shouldn't I be able to fight to have that back?"

"I'll bet you would fight." He laughed for the first time since the admission about his brother. "Bow or sword?"

"I can hold my own with a bow."

"See? That's where you differ. If it isn't a knitting needle or a paintbrush, my sisters can't wield it."

"Oh."

He grinned. "I'm not the woman-hater that you thought I was, am I? I'm just a deep, dark, tortured soul."

"You're something, alright." She busied herself making the tea while his eyes burned into her back. Her hands shook as she poured steaming water into the two chipped cups.

"I know you're used to better." She handed him a cup.

His eyes didn't leave hers. "This is perfect."

A blush rose up her cheeks as he took a sip and peered at her over the rim. She drank her tea in silence before twisting her hair into a simple braid.

He frowned and set his cup on the table.

"What's wrong?" she asked self-consciously.

"It's just …" He blew out a breath, stepping closer once again and fingering the end of her braid. "I like your hair free and wild."

"Wild?" she breathed.

He nodded.

"Do you always say whatever is on your mind to a complete stranger?"

"Oh, but you're not a stranger. You saved my life. You took care of me. I told you about my brother and I don't talk about that with anyone. There's something different about you."

Mira's chest rose and fell rapidly as Wren leaned in, so close that if she moved she'd brush up against his.

He lowered his voice. "To answer your earlier question, if I really said whatever was on my mind, I wouldn't hesitate to tell you how much I've wanted to kiss you since the first moment I saw you on the forest floor."

She sucked in a breath and waited. She wanted it just as much as he did. He'd be leaving the next day. She'd never see him again. He may be killed in the coming wars.

But none of that registered as his lips met hers. They were soft and warm and tasted like the tea she'd just served him.

Wren's arms snaked around her waist and pinned her against his hard chest. She ran her hands up over his arms, the sides of his face, into his hair. One of his hands yanked the ribbon from her hair and pulled the braid loose before he tangled his fingers in her curls.

"Mira," he groaned as he pulled away and rested his forehead against hers.

He didn't have to explain what it meant. She knew. She felt it too, an impossible weight that settled around her shoulders.

Before they could break apart, the door was flung open.

"Mira," her mother yelled. "What is the meaning of this?"

She came in followed by Mira's father and a man from the village named Hendry. Hendry was a middle-aged man who had lost his wife and child a few years before when sickness ravaged the village. He wasn't a particularly nice man or even nice looking, but he had status.

Hendry looked from Mira to Wren and his eyes narrowed before he pushed through the door to leave without a word.

Mira's mother turned on Wren. "You! We let you into our home. We give you food. How do you repay us? You take advantage of our daughter and ruin everything. I want you out. My husband will retrieve your horse. I don't care if you're well enough to travel. You will leave this village."

Mira's father went to get the horse and Wren hung his head. The smile that so often graced his face was gone, replaced by desperation.

"Mira," he started.

"I said out!" Mira's mouth pushed him towards the door. "My daughter has more important things to worry about – like if her fiancé will forgive this dalliance."

"Fiancé?" he croaked.

Mira couldn't believe what she was hearing. She met Wren's tortured gaze and shook her head. "There's no one. I promise."

Outside a horse snorted and Wren's shoulders dropped.

"He isn't well enough to ride," Mira pleaded with her mother.

"That is no longer your concern."

Wren looked up once more and gave her a final sad smile. "By tomorrow I should be strong enough. I'll just stay in the forest tonight. I'm sorry to have caused so many problems, but I do thank you for the care you gave me."

Mira choked back a sob as he disappeared out the door into the bright sunlight. A chill sank into her bones and she sat on the edge of her bed.

"Honestly, Mira," her mother scolded. "Your behavior is the reason no one wants you – until now, that is. Hendry is finally ready for a new wife and your father and I have given him your hand. Now I must go and convince him that he didn't make a grave mistake."

She rushed off and Mira buried her face in her hands to muffle her sobs. Wren's face appeared in her mind. His kind words rang in her ears. His humor warmed her heart.

All gone.

She was to marry a man who would be neither kind nor funny.

Her father returned with Tara and Toro in tow. The twins saw her tears and hugged her tightly.

Time passed and all she wanted to do was curl up and forget the day.

But she was a dutiful daughter.

She was always a good girl.

So, she got up and tamed her hair, even pinching her cheeks to give them color. Then she fixed dinner. Her mother returned as she was cutting a warm loaf of bread.

Hendry was with her. He scowled at her and took one of the only chairs that sat around the table, leaving her to stand as they ate their meager offerings.

Hendry wiped his mouth on the back of his arm. "The wedding will be in two days."

"That soon?" Mira squeaked.

"Why wait to have you warming my bed?" He rose from the chair. "You will walk me out."

Mira swallowed past the lump in her throat and set her plate down with a nod. Her mother gave her a warning look and she knew what it meant.

She was to give the man whatever he wanted.

Hendry stopped outside the door and faced her. His eyes scanned her from head to toe. "You're not quite the beauty my first wife was, but I guess you'll do." He sighed as he reached out and ran a hand across her shoulders, assessing. He moved lower, squeezing her breasts.

She held back a yelp.

His hands ran down her sides and around her back until he was gripping her buttocks. Her skin crawled as he pulled her towards him and claimed her mouth.

His kiss was not gentle as Wren's had been. It was rough as he assaulted her tongue with his. He tasted of tobacco and ale and it was all she could do not to gag.

He pushed her away from him abruptly. "Yes, you'll do nicely in my bed."

As he stalked away, a shiver ran through her. That had to have been the vilest man she'd ever met and her mother made sure she was shackled to him completely.

Was it spite? Did she really hate her that much?

That was the moment everything changed for Mira. She realized there was nothing left for her in that small village. Her mother was cruel. Her father didn't care. She would miss her brother and sister, but that wasn't enough.

She re-entered the small house and crawled into bed, pulling the covers up over her head, and waited. It took a long time for the rest of her family to settle down and go to bed.

"I just wish we could have done better for her," her father whispered in the dark.

"You're soft. Hendry is the best that girl could snag," her mother replied.

Then everything was silent as they drifted off except for the loud snores of her mother.

* * *

Mira didn't know what time it was when she snuck from her bed. Her bare feet made no sound on the dirt floor of their home as she grabbed her few possessions. By the door sat her father's beaten up weapons. They were in disrepair, but better than nothing. She grasped the curve of the bow and stuffed the pile of arrows in her bag before pulling the door open, cringing when it made a soft thud.

Looking back, they were all still sleeping. She watched their faces once more knowing that it was the last time. A part of her knew she should be sad, but this life had never felt like hers. She'd never belonged. She hiked her small bag onto her shoulder and made her way through the deserted streets as quickly as she could.

It took her about an hour to get from the village to the forest, but the excitement kept her tired legs going. It wasn't until she saw the glow of a fire that she started to run.

A form was sleeping on the ground close to the flames. Too close.

She dropped her bag and ran faster. If he rolled, his cloak could catch fire.

"Wren," she yelled as she saw the edge of his cloak burst with a tiny flame. She grabbed his water skin from the ground beside him and doused it, spraying Wren's face in the process. He woke up sputtering.

"Damn, that's cold."

"I wouldn't have had to pour it on you if you weren't sleeping so close to the fire. Do you enjoy needing someone to save your life or something?"

He grinned as he finally woke enough to realize it was her. "By you? Always." He removed his wet cloak and got to his feet. "Shouldn't you be with your fiancé?"

She scrunched up her face. "I can't marry him."

"But your parents ..."

"They don't get a say if I'm not even there for them to control."

"What do you mean?"

"I'm coming with you?"

"No."

"What?" She planted her hands on her hips. "You said it yourself that the king needs anyone who is willing to fight. Well, I'm willing."

"No."

"Is this a woman thing?" She glared. "I thought we already went over this. If you don't want me to go with you, then I'll just find my own way to the palace. I can't stay here."

She tried to stalk by him, but he grabbed her arm.

"It isn't a woman thing," he said. "I can't stand the thought of you going to war."

"And you think I like that you're going? I just met you days ago, and already I find myself worrying about something happening to you. I've never felt like this. I ..."

He cut her off with a kiss that held everything she'd been trying to say, everything she felt. He didn't argue anymore. She pulled him down near the fire – but not too near – and they kissed until they fell asleep.

The next morning, they woke in each other's arms as if that was a normal occurrence. Wren was feeling okay to ride and they both mounted the horse and set off towards the palace of Dreach-Sciene.

He was no prince. She was no princess. There would be no happy endings.

Because war was on the horizon and they'd just traded everything they were to fight for everything they believed in.

The End

About the Author: Michelle Lynn

Michelle Lynn writes many genres, mainly because her mind tends to be all over the place. She writes dystopian and contemporary romance, but her true love is fantasy. Tenelach is the follow up short story between Prophecy of Darkness and Legacy of Light in the Legends of the Tri-Gard series by M. Lynn and Michelle Bryan.

When she isn't writing, Lynn is spending time with her family in Tampa, Florida, swimming, reading, and being the major TV nerd that she is.

Books by Michelle Lynn:
Dawn of Rebellion
Day of Reckoning
Eye of Tomorrow
Choices
Promises
Dreams
We Thought We Were Invincible
We Thought We Knew It All

Links:
Facebook:
https://www.facebook.com/Michelle-Lynn-Author-706537056079631
Twitter: https://twitter.com/AuthorMichelleL
Website: http://michellelynnauthor.com/

Lightning Source UK Ltd.
Milton Keynes UK
UKHW041834260121
377731UK00001B/81